For my mother

PENGU

COLETTE

Allan Massie was born in 1938, brought up in Aberdeenshire and educated at Glenalmond and Trinity College, Cambridge. He is the author of four novels, the most recent of which was *One Night in Winter*, and of four books of non-fiction, including a study of Muriel Spark. He and his wife have three children and live in the Scottish Borders with a cat, dogs and horses.

LIVES OF MODERN WOMEN

General Editor: Emma Tennant

Lives of Modern Women is a series of short biographical portraits by distinguished writers of women whose ideas, struggles and creative talents have made a significant contribution to the way we think and live now.

It is hoped that both the fascination of comparing the aims, ideals, set-backs and achievements of those who confronted and contributed to a world in transition, and the high quality of writing and insight in these biographies, will encourage the reader to delve further into the lives and work of some of this century's most extraordinary and necessary women.

Allan Massie

Colette

Penguin Books

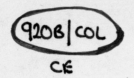

C2106 2 33 99

920B/COL

CE

Penguin Books Ltd, Harmondsworth, Middlesex, England
Penguin Books, 625 Madison Avenue, New York, New York 10022, U.S.A.
Penguin Books Australia Ltd, Ringwood, Victoria, Australia
Penguin Books Canada Limited, 2801 John Street, Markham, Ontario, Canada L3R 1B4
Penguin Books (N.Z.) Ltd, 182–190 Wairau Road, Auckland 10, New Zealand

First published 1986

REQUEST

Made and printed in Great Britain by
Richard Clay (The Chaucer Press) Ltd, Bungay, Suffolk
Typeset in Monophoto Photina
Library of Congress Catalog Card Number: 85–052211

CONTENTS

LIST OF PLATES

ACKNOWLEDGEMENTS

Colette wrote much about her own life, both in memoirs and in her fiction. I have drawn deeply, though carefully, on her autobiographical writings, always, I hope, mindful that these represent her recollections refined by time and subsequent experience. My principal debt is therefore to Colette herself; I ended by admiring her work even more than I had done when I started writing this book.

I have benefited from the insights offered in published work by Michèle Sarde, Bertrand de Jouvenel, Joanna Richardson and Kay Dick, and I owe much to Maurice Goudeket's loving portrait of his wife, *Près de Colette*. I have also depended for an understanding of French history on a variety of historians, among whom I might mention Sir Denis Brogan, Richard Cobb, Theodore Zeldin, and Norman Stone.

I owe a great debt to my wife, without whose support I would find it difficult to function, and I am grateful to Emma Tennant and Giles Gordon for their constant encouragement. My final debt is to our cat, our companion now for eleven years; my understanding and appreciation of Colette would be less if I had not known, and lived with, this cat.

1873   28 January: birth of Sidonie-Gabrielle Colette, daughter
       of Sidonie Lannoy (b. 1835), 'Sido', and Captain Jules-
       Joseph Colette (b. 1829). She had a half-sister Juliette (b.
       1859), a half-brother Achille (b. 1863) and a brother
       Léopold (b. 1868). Colette was born at Saint-Sauveur-en-
       Puisaye in Burgundy.

1890   Captain Colette bankrupt. Family move to Châtillon-
       Coligny.

1893   Marriage to Willy (Henri Gauthier-Villars, b. 1859).
       Living in Rue Jacob.

1894   The Kinceler affair. Colette seriously ill.

1895   *Claudine à l'école* being written.

1898   Willy discovers *Claudine à l'école* again.

1900   *Claudine à l'école* published. Sensational success.

1901   *Claudine à Paris*. Affair with Georgie at Bayreuth. Moves
       to Rue de Courcelles.

1902   *Claudine en ménage. Claudine à Paris* on stage, with
       Polaire. Willy takes Les Mont-Boucons for Colette. Henri
       de Jouvenel becomes editor of *Le Matin*.

1903   *Claudine s'en va.*

1904   *Minne. Dialogues des bêtes.*

1905   *Les Égarements de Minne.* Colette and Willy separate. Death of Captain Colette.

1906   Preliminary divorce measures.

1907   *La Retraite sentimentale. Le Rêve d'Égypte* scandal. Final divorce action begins. Colette on stage in *La Chair.*

1908   *Les Vrilles de la vigne.* Acting Claudine in Paris and Lyon. Summers with Missy (the Marquise de Belboeuf).

1909   *L'Ingénue libertine.*

1910   *La Vagabonde* in *La Vie parisienne.* Wins three votes for Prix Goncourt. Colette travels with Auguste Hériot, meets Henri de Jouvenel. In Brittany with Missy, takes house at Rozven. Divorce from Willy final.

1911   Affair with Henri de Jouvenel.

1912   September: death of Sido.
         December: marries Henri de Jouvenel.

1913   *L'Entrave. L'Envers du music-hall.*
         July: Colette's daughter (Bel-Gazou) born.

1914   De Jouvenel in 23rd Infantry Regiment. Colette working as nurse.

1915   In Rome and Venice.

1916   *La Paix chez les bêtes.* Film of *La Vagabonde.*

1917   Moves to 62 Boulevard Suchet, Auteuil.

1918   De Jouvenel member of Disarmament Commission, Geneva.

1919   *Mitsou.* Colette literary editor of *Le Matin.*

1920   *Chéri* serialized in *La Vie parisienne.* Bertrand de Jouvenel (b. 1903) visits Rozven. Colette Chevalier de la Légion d'Honneur.

1921   *Chéri* dramatized in collaboration with Léopold Marchand. De Jouvenel elected to Senate.

1922   *La Maison de Claudine.* Colette plays Léa in hundredth performance of *Chéri.* Henri de Jouvenel delegate to League of Nations. Colette visits Algeria with Bertrand. *Le Blé en herbe* serialized in *Le Matin,* and cut short.

1923   *Le Blé en herbe*. Colette tours with *Chéri*, lectures in
        South of France. Separation of Colette and Henri de Jou-
        venel (December).

1924   Skiing with Bertrand de Jouvenel. Ends connection with
        Le Matin. Henri de Jouvenel Minister of Education.
        Divorce proceedings.

1925   Meets Maurice Goudeket (b. 1889).

1926   *La Fin de Chéri*. Buys La Treille Muscate (St Tropez).

1927   Moves to 9 Rue de Beaujolais (entresol flat).

1928   *La Naissance du jour. Renée Vivien*. Officier de la Légion
        d'Honneur.

1929   *La Seconde. Sido*. Colette drama critic of *La Revue de
        Paris*.

1930   *Histoires pour Bel-Gazou*.

1931   Moves to Hôtel Claridge, Champs Élysées. Death of Willy.
        Lecture tours Austria/Romania.

1932   *Ces plaisirs. Le Paradis terrestre*. Colette starts Beauty
        Institute.

1933   *La Chatte*. Becomes drama critic of *Le Journal*.

1934   *Duo*. Writes dialogue for Max Ophuls's film *Divine*.

1935   Marries Maurice Goudeket. Visits New York. Henri de
        Jouvenel dies (October).

1936   *Mes apprentissages*. Commandant de la Légion d'Hon-
        neur. Elected to Académie Royale de Langue et Littéra-
        ture de Belgique. Moves to Marignan building, Champs
        Élysées.

1937   *Bella-Vista. Le Splendeur des papillons*.

1938   Visits Fez for *France-Soir*. Sells La Treille Muscate. Moves
        to 9 Rue de Beaujolais (first floor flat).

1939   *Le Toutounier*. Buys Villa Le Parc. Begins to suffer from
        arthritis.

1940   *Chambre d'hôtel*. Broadcasts to USA. Death of Léopold
        Colette.
        June: Leaves Paris on eve of German entry.
        September: Returns to Paris.

1941	*Julie de Corneilhan.*
	December: Maurice Goudeket arrested by Germans.
1942	February: Goudeket released. *De ma fenêtre.*
1943	*Le Képi.* Severe arthritis of hip.
1944	*Gigi.* Suicide of Missy.
1945	*Les Belles Saisons.* Elected to Académie Goncourt.
1946	*L'Étoile Vesper.*
1947	Now almost immobile.
1948	Publication begins of *Oeuvres complètes.*
1949	*Le Fanal bleu.* President of Académie Goncourt. *Julie de Corneilhan* filmed.
1950	*Chéri* filmed.
1951	*Gigi* on broadway. *La Seconde* filmed.
1953	Receives Grande Médaille de la Ville de Paris. Grand Officier de la Légion d'Honneur. Receives citation from the National Institute of Arts and Letters of USA.
1954	August 3: dies. Receives secular state funeral. Buried in Père Lachaise.

CHAPTER ONE

Background and Family

'*Ces plaisirs qu'on nomme, à la légère, physiques*: these pleasures lightly called physical.' Colette used the phrase first in her novel of adolescent love, *Le Blé en herbe* (*The Ripening Seed*), then as the original title of her study of lesbian affections (*The Pure and the Impure*), which, she suggested, 'will one day be recognized perhaps as my best book'. But there are pleasures other than sexual ones which may also be called physical, and these too are often dismissed lightly. Colette never makes that mistake. She is of all prose writers the most responsive to the natural world; perhaps only Proust among novelists can be compared to her; she is as alert as Tennyson to the shimmer of dew on a leaf; she is in harmony with all animal and vegetable life; no one can conjure up the taste of food like Colette; no writer can make you hungrier for whatever may be seen, touched, smelled, tasted, heard. It was natural then that she should be so alive to the joys, pains and vagaries of love; with her quick sympathy she condemns nothing but cruelty, and understands even dishonesty. Her own life was a story of varied fortune. It can be read as an example of heroic self-realization and self-emancipation, always within the context of the society of the Third French Republic. It is distorted too if it is separated from the books she wrote, because, though she was neither a natural nor, at first, a willing writer, she became completely a writer, creating for herself in her books a persona that was eventually to be inseparable from her native character. Writing became the centre of her life, its justification and comfort: 'Nobody asks you to be happy,' she said to her third husband, Maurice Goudeket. 'Work ... Do you hear me complaining?' We never do.

Colette was born in 1873 and died in 1954. Her life therefore marched alongside that of the Third Republic, which began two years before she was born, and which she survived by fourteen years. Much of the character of that despised yet remarkable regime may be found in her work. It was a bourgeois republic, and one in which private and individual concerns were respected; there was little public spirit. With a population hardly growing, with unspoiled countryside and innumerable self-sufficient small towns, France lacked the dynamism that made German society unstable. Its Republic was based on individual liberty and the theory of equality, and it had achieved an extraordinary political and social stability which was quite unaffected by the fact that the government changed almost every year. At least till 1914 it radiated self-confidence, despite the divisions that existed between clericals and anti-clericals, left and right, and in a few districts, capital and labour. These divisions provoked verbal ferocity, but this did not seriously disturb the even tenor of Parisian or, even less, provincial life. France was a rich country, social stability maintained by that very slow growth in population – a fact which differentiated it from every other European country. The French were prodigious savers: 2,000 million francs a year. The banks flourished: Paribas (the Banque de l'Union Parisien) was recording profits of 35 per cent before 1914; between 1900 and 1914 France exported 45,000 million francs of capital. Among the savers were Colette's creations, the courtesans Léa and Mme Peloux, Chéri's mother: 'Let me tell you, Madame,' said Mme Peloux, speaking to Chéri's future mother-in-law about the marriage settlement, 'that my son has never had a ha'porth of debts since he came of age and the list of his investments bought since 1910 is worth . . .' '. . . Is worth this, that, and the other,' concluded Chéri himself, disrespectfully, 'including the skin off my nose, plus the fat off my bottom . . .'; it was indeed a world, as the two Chéri novels show, in which the ladies of the *demi-monde* (Mme Peloux began in the chorus) could flourish and build up a portfolio of investments which let them keep carriages and motors, coachmen and chauffeurs, a Paris apartment and a country house.

When we think of France of this period we see it in terms of the Impressionist painters rather than the novels of Émile Zola, who admittedly presented the dark side of the picture; but fairly enough; for the bourgeoisie and the *demi-monde*, who in effect belonged to that class, life was sweet. The

17

individualistic Third Republic was a good time to be alive. Voltaire had called Henri IV the 'most French of French kings' and the Third Republic, with its millions of peasant proprietors (56 per cent of the French lived in *communes* of fewer than 2,000 inhabitants), its two million independent shopkeepers, its proliferating restaurants, was the most French of French régimes; and Colette, its poet, the most French of French writers. It is possible to imagine her contemporaries, even the half-Jewish Proust, as products of other cultures; not so Colette, she was rooted in French soil. Only in one particular was she uncharacteristic: she had no interest in general ideas. Maurice Goudeket remembered that the first time he met her at a dinner party, 'She took no part in the conversation which was bandying general ideas across the table, except once with a "why?" which challenged all that had been said, embarrassed the speakers and produced no answer.' Later he recalled

a South American woman journalist, author apparently of several large tomes, who claimed that she had come on purpose from the far-off continent to gather 'from the greatest living feminine personality' an opinion on the serious problems of the day, and on the future of civilization and written thought. She shook hands, sat down and, pencil in hand, began: 'What do you think, Madame, from the ethnological point of view of . . .'

But Colette observed that she had beautiful eyes, was wise to wear yellow, 'exactly right with your complexion', and lured her into a 'conversation concerning the butterflies of the Amazon, wild orchids, cooking perhaps . . .' The unfortunate journalist should have consulted the young Simone de Beauvoir instead, who would doubtless have supplied her with any number of general ideas.

On the other hand, Goudeket tells us, 'her way of making contact with things was through all her senses' ... 'she absolutely had to know the name of anything she was contemplating, whether animate or inanimate, and if a name was unfamiliar or escaped her, she never could rest until she had found it; not so much to store it in her memory, as because the name completed the identity of the thing in question, and was inseparable from it ...'

Is it any wonder that Colette, at once the most sensuous and exact of writers, belongs in the imagination with Renoir and Cézanne?

Anything written about Colette must begin with her mother because, for Colette, everything good came to centre in her mother; she was the touchstone. Her mother's love was the love she depended on; her mother's approval was what she sought; only her mother could cause her to lie, as we may all deceive where we most truly love; and, when she did so, it was to save her mother pain, and the act pained her herself. The relations between Sido and Colette may find a parallel in the deep love of Mme de Sévigné for her daughter, or of Mme Proust for Marcel; and though Colette could never satisfy the depths of her mother's love (as it is perhaps impossible ever to do), she had less with which to reproach herself than either Mme de Grignan or Proust.

Sido, which is how Colette always wrote of her mother,

was born in August 1835. She was Parisian by birth but was soon sent to a peasant nurse, as was often done, on a farm at Mézille in Burgundy. She was to spend most of her life in that province, and it was Colette's own calf-country, always tenderly remembered and re-created – she spoke all her life with a Burgundian accent, with the rolled 'r', not yet a feature of Northern French speech. In fact, though, Sido was a northerner. Other members of her family lived in Brussels, and she had a great love of that city with its solid bourgeois comfort. The only exotic strain was a quadroon grandfather from one of the French West Indian islands, so that Colette herself was one-sixteenth negro. ('You know,' she wrote to the poet Francis Jammes, 'I've a black stain in my blood. Does that disgust you . . .?') For all that, and for all that Burgundy is not really the South, Sido responded to the sensuous warmth of her adopted province, and Colette drank from that source too: 'it is from Sido,' Jean Charpentier wrote, 'that Mme Colette gets her spontaneity, her humour, and that instinct or divination which makes her understand both the animal and vegetable worlds.'

Sido was married twice. Her first husband was a local landowner called Jules Robineau-Duclos. He was a drunken lout whose manners were so disagreeable that he was known to his neighbours as 'The Savage'. Sido, in this marriage, was the victim of the bourgeois respect for property: arranged marriages were normal and the character of the husband might matter less than his social position or wealth. Colette could never forget that her mother's happiness had been sacrificed on this altar.

A daughter, Juliette, was born in 1859; a son, Achille, four years later. It was rumoured (even in the prefectorial records) that Duclos was not the father of this second child. By this time his drunkenness was notorious and may have deranged his wits. He had certainly assaulted his wife more than once. Nevertheless, in conversation with Colette, Sido tenderly recalled an occasion when he had gone out of his way to find her a present: 'the Savage, who had never known how to give, did bring them to me ... as proud and clumsy as a big dog with a small slipper in his mouth'. And she kept the presents, 'a little mortar of rarest marble, for pounding almonds and sweetmeats, and a cashmere shawl', 'with sentimental care'; Colette, when she recorded the memory in the 1920s, could still make 'almond paste with sugar and lemon peel in the now cracked and dingy mortar', but reproached herself 'for having cut up the cherry-coloured shawl to make cushion covers and vanity bags'.

Duclos died in January 1865. That December Sido married Jules-Joseph Colette, who may have been Achille's father. He was a retired officer who had served in the Crimea and the Italian campaign of 1859, in which he had lost a leg – 'mother and daughter are doing fine', he said after the amputation. As a Republican and anti-clerical – he was to stand for election to the Assembly after the fall of the Second Empire in 1870–71 – he may have been in sympathy with Napoleon III's support for the cause of a United Italy against Austria and the Pope; nevertheless it cost him his leg. In compensation, as a wounded veteran, he was appointed an Inspector of Taxes. In that happier society the post was not

21

demanding, which was just as well, because Captain Colette was far from efficient. Before long he was living, apparently contentedly, on the rents from his wife's property inherited from his predecessor.

Their first child, at any rate the first born in wedlock, Léopold, arrived in 1868. Their second, our Colette, christened Sidonie-Gabrielle, was born on 28 January 1873. No childhood was to be more sheltered, delightful or happily remembered than Colette's; not even Proust's. They had much in common, these writers who were almost exact contemporaries, Proust being born in 1870. For both, childhood offered a paradise which coloured and fortified the rest of their lives. It was to be an Eden never more than half lost, which could be re-animated by the imagination and exercise of memory:

At half past three everything slumbered still in a primal blue, blurred and dewy, and, as I went down the sandy road the mist, grounded by its own weight, bathed first my legs, then my well built little body, reaching at last to my mouth and my ears, and finally to that most sensitive part of all, my nostrils. I went alone, for there were no dangers in that free-thinking countryside. It was on that road and at that hour that I first became aware of my own self, experienced an inexpressible state of grace, and felt one with the first breath of air that stirred, the first bird, and the sun so newly born that it looked not quite round.

'Beauty' my mother would call me, and 'Jewel of pure gold'; then she would let me go, watching her creation – her masterpiece, as she said – grow smaller as I ran down the road. I may have been pretty; my mother and the pictures of me at that period do not always agree. But what made me pretty at that moment was my youth and the dawn, my blue eyes deepened by the greenery all round me, my fair locks that would only be brushed smooth on my return, and my pride at being awake when other children were asleep . . .

There were 'two hidden springs which I worshipped . . . The first spring tasted of oak-leaves, the second of iron and hyacinth stalks. The mere mention of them makes me hope that their savour may fill my mouth when my time comes, and that I may carry hence with me that imagined draught . . .'

No wonder, with such a foundation, that Colette developed strong, resilient, with a character able to accommodate any number of shifts of fortune, able to absorb and value properly whatever befell her.

She had never reason to question her mother's love. 'When you came into the world, my last born, my Minet-Chérie,' Sido would say, 'I suffered for three days and two nights. When I was carrying you I was as big as a house. Three days seems a long time. The beasts put us to shame, we women who can no longer bear our children joyfully. But I've never regretted my suffering. They do say that children like you, who have been carried so high in the womb and have taken so long to come down into the daylight, are always the children the most loved, because they have lain so near their mother's heart and have been so unwilling to leave her . . .'

Perhaps she did not speak exactly like that, in so many

23

words. Colette's autobiographical memories are reconstructed with a deal of art, and it is of course unlikely that she remembered thirty or more years later her mother's precise words. Yet who can doubt that she recalled here the essence of what Sido said, and that her absolute confidence, her ability so be so truly herself, rested in her unwavering certainty that she had been loved as a child?

The upbringing Sido gave her provided her with a scale of values, acted as a talisman against the ephemeral glitter of the adult world she would enter:

Even if I had not inherited it from her, she would, I think, have given me a love for the provinces, if by province one understands not merely a place or a region distant from the capital, but a strong sense of the social hierarchy, of the necessity for irreproachable conduct, and pride at inhabiting an ancient and honoured dwelling, closed on all sides, but capable of opening at any moment on to its lofty barns, its well-filled hayloft, and its masters apt for the uses and dignity of their house . . .

Much was made in late nineteenth-century France of the contrast between north and south. Alphonse Daudet popularized a stereotype of the southerner, the man from the Midi, in his *Tartarin* books: he was a creature of impulse and strong passions, whereas the northerner was supposed to be colder and more ratiocinative. Since Captain Colette was a Provençal, Colette might be thought to have inherited both strains. Yet though she may be regarded as southern in her sensuous responsiveness, northern in her good sense and dogged application, in her case the stereotype breaks down.

By her own account, and in the view of her friends, she features as almost wholly Sido's daughter; Captain Colette remains a marginal figure.

'It seems strange to me,' she wrote in 1929, 'that I knew him so little. My attention, my fervent attention, were all for Sido and only fitfully strayed from her. It was just the same with my father. His eyes dwelt on Sido. On thinking it over I believe that she did not know him well either.' Colette speaks of his 'boundless generosity', his 'childish confidence', his 'sham southern rages' – 'Italian! Knife-man!' Sido used to say mockingly. He lived much in his imagination, and Colette could distinguish her father's 'lyricism' in herself. But she did not know him well and came to regret it. She 'could paint from memory the climbing rose and the trellis that supported it, as well as the hole in the wall and the worn flagstone. But I can only see my father's face vaguely and intermittently ... elsewhere he is a wandering, floating figure, full of gaps, obscured by clouds and visible only in patches.' Still she did inherit one other characteristic: his rages. These could seem tremendous: 'one has only to go to Saint-Sauveur, and see the state to which my father reduced the marble chimney-piece there, with two kicks from his one foot'; surely a remarkable acrobatic achievement.

Sido's luminous magnetism destroyed any chance of a full, even normal, relationship developing between father and daughter. How could it do so, when both were obsessed with her? 'All we four children certainly made my father uncomfortable. How can it be otherwise in families where the father, though almost past the age for passion, remains in love with his mate? All his life long we disturbed the tête-à-tête of which he had dreamed.' Consequently, jealousy simmered, of an unusual sort. It is common for a daughter to feel her mother a rival for her father's love. Colette reversed the norm. For her, the father was the rival. The family situation in short was that which Freud saw as likely to produce a homosexual son. Later, Colette's stepson, Renaud de Jouvenel, was to suggest that the image of the one-legged Captain making love to Sido aroused in Colette a distaste for normal sexual relations. There is no evidence to support this claim, but the dominant role that Sido played, and in memory and imagination continued to play, in Colette's life, at least until the 1920s when she treated of it fully in two books, may have distorted her other loving relations, may account in part for the course taken by her three marriages, two of which were strangely unequal, two unsatisfactory, and also for the curiously incomplete relationship with her own daughter.

Nevertheless, being in the company of one she adored, in an enchanted garden and a house she loved equally deeply, Colette's childhood was happy. Two events cast a shadow over it, however; in both she was an observer, not an actor.

First, in 1885, her half-sister Juliette married a local doctor. It was her own choice and it turned out unhappily, for Captain Colette's mismanagement of his wife's property had already gone so far that he was unable to fulfil the terms of the marriage contract and pay the agreed dowry. Juliette's husband and new family found this intolerable.

They forbade her to speak to her own family again, a prohibition all the more painful because they in fact lived next door. Eventually Juliette tried to kill herself. A neighbour came to tell Sido. She was helpless in her grief. The Captain's response thrilled the young Colette: though he had never grown fond of Juliette, the sight of Sido's misery enraged him: 'Without raising his voice, and in his most honeyed tones, my father said: "Go and tell my daughter's husband, tell Doctor R, that if he does not save that child, by evening he will have ceased to live." ' This was fine Southern melodrama, doubtless sincere; it could hardly soothe Sido. There was a common belief that, despite the patriarchal attitudes of the law, Frenchwomen in reality often played the dominant role in their household. No doubt this was true in many cases. Juliette's marriage, however, taught Colette how wretchedly dependent women could be, and how great unhappiness could be caused by their subservient position; it gave her too a scunner at the bourgeois, one might say Forsyte, tendency to regard marriage as an affair of property; to see a wife as her husband's possession.

Then, five years later, the Captain's incapacity in financial matters brought his family to disaster. The details are unimportant: he had remitted rents, on pleas of poverty, and then borrowed to make good the deficiency, till he found himself sinking in a morass of debt. Their house had to be sold; even the property put up to public auction. The humiliation was extreme. Yet Colette was to draw strength from it in time. Apart from this, she said, her life before her marriage was 'roses all the way; yet what would I have done with a life that was nothing but roses?' Possibly some experience of asperity is required if a happy childhood is to be fully appreciated or even fruitful; otherwise it can be, in the words of Colette's biographer, Michèle Sarde, 'a poor preparation for human contacts'.

The Captain too was resilient under the disaster. He had always been so. Colette came to admire this quality in him. At the time, she was to reflect,

he was not only misunderstood, but unappreciated. 'That incorrigible gaiety of yours!' my mother would exclaim, not in reproach but astonishment. She thought he was gay because he sang. But I who whistle whenever I am sad, and turn the pulsations of fever, or the syllables of a name that torments me, into endless variations on a theme, could wish she had understood that pity is the supreme insult. My father and I have no use for pity; our nature rejects it. And now the thought of my father tortures me, because I know he possessed a virtue more precious than any facile charms; that of knowing full well why he was sad, and never revealing it . . .

'Wherever he went,' she wrote, 'his song preceded and protected him.'

He lived a dozen years after the crash; they went to stay with Achille, now a doctor. The Captain spent much of his time in his study, working on books. None was ever submitted to a publisher, but when he died bound copies were found on the shelves. They bore such titles as 'My Campaigns', 'The Lessons of 1870', and 'Marshal MacMahon as seen by a comrade-in-arms'. Each was dedicated to Sido;

but there was no text beyond the dedication. The bound pages of 'beautiful, cream-laid paper or thick foolscap' were blank; 'imaginary works, the mirage of a writer's career'.

CHAPTER TWO

Willy

Colette married on 15 May 1893. She was just twenty and quite inexperienced, in worldly terms young for her age, for she knew little beyond her Burgundian village and loving family. In marrying, she exchanged the country for Paris, and the house of a father who was an imaginary author for the flat of a husband who practised what in Captain Colette was a harmless little deception on a far grander and more ambitious scale. His name was Henri Gauthier-Villars, but everyone knew him as Willy. He was fourteen years older than Colette, and already notorious. Raymond Escolier was later to describe him as 'repulsive: one of the most putrid wrecks of the *belle époque*', but the novelist J.-H. Rosny was bewildered by his charm and found 'his ascendancy extraordinary'.

He was the son of Albert Gauthier-Villars, a publisher specializing in scientific works. This Gauthier-Villars had been one year ahead of Captain Colette at the military academy of St-Cyr; like him he had served in the Crimean and Italian campaigns; they were both members of the Société de Géographie. The young Willy was conventionally educated at the Lycée Condorcet and the Collège Stanislas. In 1878, aged nineteen, he published a book of sonnets, which appear to have been his own work; the action disturbed his father, who feared that he might have a poet to support. (Later Willy was to point to a purple passage in one of Colette's early pieces and ask scathingly, 'Have I married the last of the lyric poets?') However, in 1880 he was called up for military service and became a second lieutenant in the same regiment as Alfred Dreyfus, not yet the most inescapable name in France.

Released from the army, Willy abandoned sonnets (no money in them) and embarked on the muddy waters of literary journalism and miscellaneous hackwork. The years between 1880 and 1914 were the great age of journalism in France as in England. It was cheap to start and run a paper; consequently new titles flooded on to the market. Paris alone boasted more than seventy daily papers in 1900. In France there were 2,857 newspapers and periodicals in 1900, 3,442 in 1904. Books proliferated in the same manner, tumbling from the press in a couple of weeks. The printed word had no rival as a means of disseminating information and judgement. Willy plunged into the stream with a zest that belonged to the times and an ingenuity that was all his own.

He set up as a music critic, though he had only a general superficial knowledge of the art. That did not matter. Cleverer than others who have found themselves in this position, he took care to be well primed with musical terms by friends such as Debussy. These lent his pieces a spurious authority, but he soon hit on a happy and original vein: 'My notion,' he said later, 'was to devise a gay mocking witty column that would make pleasant reading!' He devised for himself the persona of an usherette – *'Une ouvreuse du cirque d'été'* – who allowed herself free comment on concerts as newsworthy occasions as well as on the music played. 'She' was outspoken and scandalous, and, since her identity was hardly a secret (which would have dulled the joke), Willy's reputation bloomed, and he acquired enemies, indispensable for the self-publicist. Once, for example, he was assaulted before a concert by the composer Erik Satie; the usherette remarked, 'I was distracted during the first part of the symphony, involved as I was in the sight of M. Erik Satie being beaten with a stick.' That Willy himself was wielding the stick added to the author's furtive pleasure.

Before long, however, he realized that others could do more than supply information; they could actually write the stuff. The Willy factory was founded. Since it was the exist-ence of this factory that determined Colette's career as a writer, it merits a little attention. Willy set up as a literary capitalist, an entrepreneur of letters who would supply columns, essays, paragraphs of gossip, dialogues and, in time, complete novels and books of scandalous history and spurious memoirs; and of these he would write hardly a line himself. He was a natural slave-driver – appropriately, the French for a literary ghost who writes books or articles to which another puts his name is 'un nègre'. 'We,' Colette wrote in *Mes apprentissages*, 'the veterans of the old gang –

Pierre Veber, Vuillemoz, that excellent fellow "Cur", Prince of Gastronomes Marcel Boulestin and myself – whenever we meet and talk of our duped and despoiled past, we always say: "in the days when we worked in the factory".'

Such entrepreneurs were nothing new. Alexandre Dumas, for instance, had employed his teams of *'nègres'*. What was remarkable about Willy was his own utter aversion from writing. His was not the case, as Colette saw it, 'of an ordinary man who engaged other men to write the books he signed'; it had 'one unique and remarkable feature; the man who did not write was more talented than the men who wrote in his stead'. Yet, Colette goes on, 'between the wish, the need to produce saleable printed matter, and the art of writing, this strange author encountered an obstacle I have never been able to picture – some barrier of a peculiar shape and quality, unknown, possibly terrifying.' We are all familiar with ghosted work, and usually a ghost is employed because the nominal author has no concept of how a book should be made. But Willy knew this very well. His instructions to his scribes were precise, detailed, copious and intelligent; they might be, so Colette tells us, 'as long as, if not longer than, the required paragraph', and yet that paragraph, that essay, that sketch, that novel, which he so minutely described, often to more than one ghost, for several drafts might require several hands, was just what he could not bring himself to do. He must have spent more hours cajoling work from others, and criticizing that work and indicating how it must be revised, than would have been needed to do the piece in the first instance. That, however, could not be done. Colette speaks of 'an undeniable condition of morbid laziness and a timidity of expression'. Yet perhaps the pleasures of intrigue and organizing others played an equal part.

This was the strange creature Colette had married. How did such an odd and unexpected union come about? A tentative answer may be given in three words: accident, propinquity, hunger.

Accident: in 1889 Willy's mistress had a child called Jacques. The mother died two years later. The child was sickly. The doctors recommended country air and country food. Casting around for someone on whom he could impose his young son, Willy hit on the wife of his father's old friend Captain Colette. Sido assented and took the child in the spring of 1892.

Propinquity: Willy visited his child – Burgundy was charming, just the right distance from Paris, for a trip to the country. He met the beautiful nineteen-year-old girl with her marvellous hair, and ... it is hard to say what: undoubtedly her beauty attracted him, perhaps her inexperience appealed to the timidity that lurked beneath the flamboyant swagger of his manner, and which made him shrink from a relationship with his equal. At any rate, she was invited to Paris; he proposed and was accepted.

Hunger: Colette was later to reproach herself, seeing her marriage as the fruit of

a guilty rapture, an atrocious impure adolescent impulse. There are many scarcely nubile girls who dream of becoming the show, the plaything, the licentious masterpiece of some middle-aged man. It is an ugly dream that is punished by its fulfilment, a morbid thing, akin to the neuroses of puberty, the habit of eating chalk and coal, of drinking mouthwash, of reading dirty books and sticking pins into the palm of your hand.

There is a wealth of self-disgust here; yet at the time there can be no doubt that Colette wanted what she got. She was dazzled by Willy and infatuated with him. It is clear too, that, whatever the family circumstances, whatever the attractions of a husband of good birth and apparently sound financial standing might be to an impoverished family which could not supply a dowry, and which had already suffered, in Juliette's case, from their inability to do so, Sido would never have pushed her beloved daughter into a marriage that was repugnant to her. As it was, she had doubts: the courtship was disturbed by anonymous letters denouncing Willy's way of life, and the presence of the young Jacques can hardly have been reassuring. 'No, we haven't had any more anonymous letters,' Sido wrote to Juliette just before the marriage. One can read an effort to maintain her equanimity into the words: 'Willy surprised her,' she said, 'he showed her their future apartment, completely furnished down to the row of shining pots and pans ready to be cooked in tomorrow.' Someone was deceiving here, for there was in fact no kitchen in Willy's bachelor apartment where they first lived.

There are two scenes in Colette's fiction, written more than forty years apart, which reproduce a situation like her own, and indicate the depths of her self-disgust. In *Claudine*

à Paris and *Gigi*, a young girl, in love with a middle-aged
man, desperate to win him, offers herself as his mistress;
and in both cases it is the man who holds out for marriage.
There is no reason to suppose that this scene, which reverses
a convention of fiction and the theatre, represents what
actually happened between Colette and Willy. Yet it is
psychologically true, and it was Colette's realization of this
which disgusted her.

Yet she only felt that in retrospect. At the time she loved
Willy. In a letter to Proust, for instance, written in the
spring of 1895, she wrote: 'I feel that you understand me
perfectly, because, as your letter shows, you know that my
Willy is an original mind . . . it seems to me that we have
quite a few tastes in common, a taste for Willy among
others.' Yet the desire, love, admiration that she felt could
not make her happy . . .

Naturally they must live in Paris. Willy could not be
imagined away from Montmartre. He was a true creature of
the *belle époque*, with all its seedy glitter, this prematurely
old-looking, fleshy, bald and affected figure. 'It has been said
that he bore a marked resemblance to Edward VII,' his wife
recalled. 'To do justice to a less flattering but no less august
truth, I would say that, in fact, the resemblance was to
Queen Victoria'; moreover, as she was 'the Mother of
Europe', Willy was the mother of cheap journalism and
risqué fiction. He was addicted to Bohemia; as for Colette,
'what is known as the Bohemian life has always suited me
about as badly as a hat trimmed with ostrich feathers or a

pair of ear-rings. I do not mean the sort of "Bohemia" I organized for myself when the time came. That Bohemia could have given points for hard work and almost finical punctuality to any storekeeper's staff.'

It was a Paris still innocent of the motor-car and where the Métro was hardly under construction and not opened till 1901. The Eiffel Tower was only four years old; Maxim's, that restaurant which expressed the essence of the *belle époque*, opened in the year of their marriage. The old aristocracies had lost political power: 'France,' writes Norman Stone, 'stood out in Europe of the late nineteenth century as the only country where aristocracy was not predominant in politics ... even French ambassadors were sometimes middle-class ... the Third Republic catered for the responsible self-government of the self-reliant individual.' It was, in short, a world made safe for Willy; though the aristocracy, as readers of Proust know, still flourished socially, it overlapped with the *demi-monde*, and the painter and man of letters Jacques-Émile Blanche observed that 'this singular couple, Willy and Colette, moved in the best, and the worst, society ...'

They lived first in Willy's bachelor flat in the Rue Jacob, above the Gauthier-Villars publishing offices. It was, in Colette's memory, 'a quaking echoing garret at the top of one of the houses on the quays ... soaked in a sort of horrible office gloom. Heaps of yellowing newspapers occupied the chairs; German postcards were strewn everywhere, celebrating the attractions of underclothes, socks, ribboned drawers and buttocks.' This gloomy salacity reflected Willy's taste: one of the Willy novels, *Suzette veut me lâcher*, opens with the line: 'Marquise, why are you putting your knickers on again?' There was, as I have said, no kitchen; the young Colette was deprived of even the most sacred territory of the French wife. It was a relief to cross the river in the morning and breakfast in a milkshop on 'rolls dipped in pale mauve chocolate'.

She was of course quite unprepared for Paris or Willy's sort of life. She had, as it were, fallen in it, as Alice fell down the rabbit hole. She was lonely, unhappy, neglected and confused, kept as a species of pet by Willy, one who was to be thrown a crust from time to time. When they moved to another flat, also in the Rue Jacob, there was nothing to lift her depression. The sun never shone in those four rooms; her friend, the Comédie Française actress Marguerite Moreno, remembered that 'when I first met you, you were living in an "almost" old apartment . . . there was a gloomy courtyard, a vast chilling stairway and a kitchen on the landing across from your apartment . . .' Worse, it had been occupied for more than fifty years by an eccentric tenant whose idea of decoration had been to cover every available inch with 'tiny diamond-shaped confetti of many colours' – more than 275,000 pieces, according to the concierge.

She had no friends of her own age. Sometimes in the evenings Willy would drag her to the offices of *L'Écho de Paris*, where she would spend hours sitting on a bench while he waited to correct the proofs of an article. Then, 'Aren't you dying of thirst?', Willy would say, and take her off to the Brasserie Gambrinus, though in fact she was dying for sleep. There she would sit through the night sipping her lemonade and red-currant syrup (Colette was always abstemious), while Willy, as a good Wagnerian and German-fancier, drank beer. Not much of a life for a young girl, one might think.

She was kept short of money, for Willy, obsessed with his finances, was mean. Sido, arriving on a visit, was horrified to discover that her daughter had no overcoat. 'She said nothing. She gave her son-in-law a look out of keen wide eyes, and took me off to the Magasins du Louvre to buy a black coat, trimmed with "Mongolian" fur that cost one hundred and twenty-five francs and seemed to me sumptuous.' Yet she could not speak frankly to Sido now; for the thirteen years of her marriage, she pretended that she was happy.

In 1895 she fell ill. The cause may have been psychosomatic; nevertheless she nearly died. As she saw it later, 'There is always a moment in the lives of the very young when death seems as natural and attractive as life.' Dr Jullien, 'the great Saint-Lazare physician', wrote to tell Sido that he was afraid he would not be able to save her daughter. At once she hurried to the rescue: 'No doubt she toiled, day and night, dragging me back from the threshold she would not have me cross.' Colette was confined to bed for two months. Only when she was on her feet again did Sido return to Burgundy 'where the Captain waited and pined'. Colette now remarked 'the singular invariable coolness' her mother displayed to 'the man she always called

Monsieur Willy'. If death had been a temptation in this illness, it was one which would never threaten Colette again; perhaps her reverence for life was confirmed by the glimpse across that threshold from which Sido had restrained her.

She began now to acquire friends. They were mostly of her husband's generation, for she met them through him, and mostly writers. She was closest to two talented eccentrics: Marcel Schwob, who later married Marguerite Moreno, herself to be Colette's lifelong friend, and Paul Masson, whom she was to use as the model for the character of Masseau in *L'Entrave*. Masson was a former colonial magistrate, an inveterate punster and practical joker, who smoked opium and later killed himself – the incidence of suicide was high among the denizens of the *belle époque*. Schwob, learned, a Sinophile and novelist of some talent, would come to her bedside and read for hours from English and American books which he was translating: Dickens, Twain, Defoe, Jerome K. Jerome. (Her taste in English literature would later run more to Conrad and Kipling.) She considered that he 'wasted his time on me with superb generosity', of which she only became fully conscious later.

No doubt the friends were attracted by her beauty, her innocence, her apparent helplessness; no doubt their jaded palates were refreshed by her spontaneity. Almost certainly they discerned in Colette qualities of which she was herself ignorant. There were after all plenty of pretty girls in Montmartre with whom they might occupy themselves. But, making no advances to Colette, they sought out her company and spent hours with her. Pity for her unhappy condition is an inadequate explanation.

Her emancipation from Willy began with an anonymous letter – 'anonymous letters often tell the truth'. Following its suggestion, she took a cab to the Rue Bochard-de-Saron, rang the bell of a tiny mezzanine-floor flat, and there discovered her husband with a pretty, if very small, young woman. She did not exactly take them *in flagrante delicto*, for they were in fact poring over Willy's sacred account book. Yet all three recognized that Willy and Charlotte Kinceler had been caught in complicity. Though Colette's immediate reaction was that this too must be hidden from Sido, the effect of the discovery was liberating; it loosened the chain forged by her 'atrocious adolescent impulse'. Later she came to know Charlotte; they were 'courteous, like duellists after a fight'. She would call on her in the herbalists' shop she started in the Rue Pauquet, and drink lime-flower tea. So she learned of Charlotte's abrupt infatuation with the idea of salvation, of the torrid confessionals to which 'she went as she would have swallowed a drink in a public-house on a very thirsty day'. She became aware of the strange stresses and contradictions in this 'fresh-looking and tainted' girl who had seemed to her 'the first young priestess of the new-born convention that was Montmartre'; who was made the subject of a play by Brieux, and who dazzled and seduced writers like Lucien Guitry and Jules Lemaître; and who 'one afternoon of stifling summer rain went into her back-shop parlour and shot herself through the mouth. She was twenty-six and had saved money', and Montmartre was a more tortured and complicated place than the tourists who already frequented it in search of 'life' supposed.

Her second act of emancipation seemed first a chain binding her more tightly to Willy. One day he suggested to her that, money being short – 'Quick, dear, there's not a sou in the house' was his catchphrase – she might perhaps set down her memories of her school days. There was a market for such stuff, the spicier the better. Obediently she set to work, wrote her piece, and was unconcerned when her lord and master found it not to his purpose. He shoved it away in a drawer and forgot about it until, a couple of years later, he was tidying up his desk. All at once, some episode, some observation, some trick of style, caught his attention. He stiffened. 'What a fool I have been,' he muttered, and dashed off to the printer's.

So – it is now one of the most famous of French literary anecdotes, to be set beside Céleste Albaret's story of how the *Nouvelle revue française* returned *Du côté de chez Swann* to Proust, with the peculiar knots with which she had tied the packet that contained the manuscript never having been undone, because, it seems, André Gide had assured everyone that 'a little socialite like Monsieur Proust could not write a novel of any interest' – so, Claudine was born, and so Colette became a writer. She had had no literary ambitions; she had merely obeyed her husband; but, with his recognition of the quality of the manuscript, she had entered the factory, been recruited to the chain-gang, found, unsuspectingly, her *métier*. For the novel was, of course, published, with Willy's name as author, and he revelled in its success. He did not deny its true author all credit: 'He got into the habit of making me listen to the lavish compliments that were paid him, of laying his soft hand on my head, of saying: "but you know this child has been most precious to me. Oh yes, she has! She has told me the most delicious things about her school." '

There were to be four true Claudine novels: *Claudine à l'école* (*Claudine at School*), *Claudine à Paris* (*Claudine in Paris*), *Claudine en ménage* (*Claudine Married*), and *Claudine s'en va* (*Claudine and Annie*). (Later, after the break with Willy, there was also *La Retraite sentimentale* (*Retreat from Love*) and, in 1922, *La Maison de Claudine*, but this book, published in English as *My Mother's House*, has nothing at all to do with the fictional character, Claudine.) They had straight away an extraordinary success, the first selling 40,000 copies in two months. Willy swelled like a balloon. Claudine was the sensation of the town; he had never experienced anything like it . . . There were Claudine lotions, Claudine ice-cream, Claudine scent. A shop called La Samaritaine sold Claudine collars and Claudine hats and Willy rice-powder. There were even Claudine cigarettes, and postcards were sold of Willy with Claudine (Colette), she wearing button boots and a schoolgirl dress. It was said that only God, and perhaps Captain Dreyfus, were more famous. When *Claudine in Paris* was dramatized, with a remarkable performance in the name part by a young actress called Polaire, Willy insisted that Colette cut her hair (to Sido's indignant dismay), so that she and Polaire would look like twins. In short, he was ready to use every trick of publicity in order to exploit the books' vogue. He was even prepared to let it be said that Colette and Polaire re-enacted the schoolgirl passions portrayed in the novels, though the robust American lesbian Nathalie Clifford Barney declared they were 'passions which neither Colette nor Polaire felt for each other'.

Willy and Colette became the most famous couple in Paris. Jean Cocteau recalled their appearance.

Round one of the tables sat Willy, Colette and her bulldog. Willy, with his thick moustache, his eyes gleaming under his heavy lids, his fancy cravat, his top-hat on its cardboard halo, his bishop's hands folded on the knob of his cane . . . Beside him, our Colette. Not the solid Colette who offers us succulent salads with raw onions and does her shopping in sandals at Hédiard. No, it was a thin, thin Colette, a kind of little fox in cycling dress, a fox-terrier in skirts.

Some, knowing their Willy, suspected what had happened. The poet Catulle Mendès said to Colette:

You wrote the *Claudines*, didn't you. That's all right, you needn't overdo the bashfulness. In – in I don't know how long – in twenty years, perhaps thirty, people will find out. And then you will see what it means for a writer to have created a type. You don't realize it now. Oh, it's a big thing! But it's a sort of punishment too, a guilt that follows you everywhere, that sticks to your skin – a reward that becomes intolerable, that you want to spew up . . .

She remembered these words, for her own judgement of the *Claudines* was severe, though she was to come to resent Willy's theft of her work, and even more perhaps the folly with which he sold the copyrights and so deprived her of future returns, until she had to go to the courts to establish her authorship. Even so, there have always remained those, both detractors and admirers of Colette, who have claimed that the *Claudine* books were the result of collaboration. So Pierre d'Hollander maintained that in his opinion 'Willy personally made many corrections in the MS after he re-discovered it.' That, or the reworking of the material by another hand, would certainly have been in accordance with his normal practice, and Colette's warmest admirers, dismayed by the sly and knowing vulgarity that pervades the *Claudine* books (and is found nowhere else in her work), may wish to believe it. Yet she herself maintained that they were almost entirely her own work, and, since she was hardly proud of them, finding in them certain things which 'betray an utter disregard of doing harm', one can believe her.

The *Claudine* books still throb with a surge of life, but there is an inescapable cheapness in them. They have a whiff of the mean and fleshy corruptness of Willy; they set out to titillate, like his German postcards. There are flashes of disagreeable anti-semitism – these Willy may have inserted, like the hardly veiled and hostile references to Madame Arman de Cavaillet, Anatole France's mistress and a model for Proust's Madame Verdurin; but one fears that Colette, knowing what was expected of her, produced them herself; they would only have echoed the sentiments she heard every day from the anti-Dreyfusard *demi-monde* who swirled round Willy, a society where even Catulle Mendès, a

kind and admirable man, could wonder whether the Jews
had ever produced an original genius, and being faced with
Spinoza, mutter, 'Spinoza? Hm, I'm not so sure about his
mother.' A sniggering triviality runs through the books,
giving them 'the Willy touch'; he even intrudes as a character; Maugis, 'all lit up with fatherly vice', with Willy's own
manner of speech, full of puns and archaic expressions, had
already been used in newspaper paragraphs and spicy
stories. Though 'no creation of mine', he forced his way into
the *Claudine* books, an emblem of Willy's galloping self-
infatuation. What redeems the books and makes them still
readable is the vivacity of the style, the dash of Claudine
herself, the occasional illuminating and natural touches,
the ability, so peculiarly Colette's and already evident, to
catch the mood of a moment before it evaporates; and yes,
beneath the contrived naughtiness, there is an essential
good humour and kindness. All this is not enough; there is
still something displeasing, faintly disgusting about the
Claudine books; they are written by a child pretending to be
corrupt. The contrast between the too-knowing tone, the
gameyness of Maugis-Willy and the cheap emotion on the
one hand, and what one senses to be the real innocence
and goodness of the true author on the other, is disquiet-
ing and ugly. Not for the first time one feels that the marriage between Willy and Colette was a subject for Henry
James.

Nevertheless Claudine was to be the means of her liber-
ation. There were two identifiable stages. In 1901 she
accompanied Willy on his annual pilgrimage to Bayreuth.

(The usherette still functioned.) There Willy had a new mistress, an American girl called Georgie Raoul-Duval. It was soon evident that Georgie was attracted to Colette too. Willy encouraged the attachment; anything to add spice and complication. The relationship is reproduced in *Claudine en ménage*, where Claudine has an affair with her husband's mistress Reza. This was hardly Claudine's first experience of lesbian love, but the affair with Reza is treated with an honesty, a seriousness and maturity not applied to Claudine's earlier frolics. Something real and enlivening had happened to her creator, though some years were to pass before Colette would pursue this line of development.

That is not surprising. She had little knowledge of women, even little acquaintance. She had never had the girl-friends most young women have known. Her confidants since her marriage had been Willy's contemporaries, or his young secretaries, some of whom, like Marcel Boulestin, the future restaurateur, were homosexuals of the type that has a feminine delicacy. (It was Boulestin who provoked one of Willy's few good jokes. He had written a novel about the homosexual underworld. It was translated into English, but the book invited prosecution in both countries. Willy suggested the French version be published in England, the English in France: 'Judges,' he explained, 'are never polyglottal; pansies always are.') Colette used Boulestin as the model for Claudine's homosexual stepson. This was, as she later saw it, an expression of her growing sense of what she had missed: female companionship and young love. Now she felt that 'as long as I debased them, I could praise the looks of a young male and speak covertly of a secret danger, an un-acknowledged attraction'. Her sense of deprivation shar-pened when she heard Polaire talk of her lover: 'Oh Colette, he does smell lovely, that young brute. And his skin! And his teeth! You just don't know.' 'No,' she could only reflect, 'I just didn't know, I who had never – for the best of reasons – known the feel of a lover's hair.'

She was being made aware of the strangeness of her marriage, of what it failed to give her. There is a curious apprehension of this in the *Claudine* books: whereas in real life Willy addressed Colette formally as *'vous'* while she called him *'tu'*, in the books the situation is reversed: Renaud says *'tu'* to Claudine, and she replies with *'vous'*. It was a marriage so incomplete that even equality of address was unat-tainable. It had, in its curious course, prolonged her ado-lescence. In doing so it represented a hard school. It taught her to know deceit and exploitation. At the same time it taught her her *métier*, so that she learned to apply herself to work with 'the slow, plodding, clerk-like determination which has never left me'. Yet, because she was denied so much, because there could be nothing easy and natural in her relations with her husband, her emotional development was retarded even while the marriage opened a window on a wider and more varied world than she could have en-countered in her native Burgundy. It saved her from the narrow self-righteous self-assurance of the provincial bour-geois; she learned from their varied acquaintance (as she was to learn still more in the next stages of her life) that much which the world condemns may exist alongside true goodness of heart, courage and loyalty. Her understanding of life, her deep sympathy were founded in this strange marriage and the world Willy led her into. Yet, in so many ways, her deprivation was real. Speaking of herself at the age of thirty, she noted her 'unusual dearth of feminine companions, of feminine complicity and support ... Not that I disliked women particularly but I was boyish and at ease in the society of men, and I feared women.'

But the success of the *Claudines* opened her prison door. The second stage was Willy's realization that she had become a valuable property, something worth more than his usual *nègre*, and might with advantage benefit from a bit of cosseting. First he gave her, for the first time since they were married, a sort of allowance – 300 francs a month bonus (except in the summer when she wouldn't be working). You could buy a lot then for 300 francs – the annual rent for their apartment in the Rue Jacob had been 1400. Now it was her turn to give presents to Sido: 'sticks of pure cocoa from Hédiard, a quilted bed-jacket, fine wool stockings, books'. Even so, 'my supreme gift to her was a lie: my pretence of happiness'.

Yet she took one small step towards achieving this in 1902. She persuaded Willy to take a house in the country for her. Les Mont-Boucons, with a little farm and a dozen acres, was in the Franche-Comté, a house in the style of the *Directoire*, though probably, Colette thought – styles coming later in the country – in reality dating from the reign of Charles X (1824–30), about thirty years later. She imagined in her innocence that the house was really hers; three years

49

later he took it away again, assuring her that in fact it belonged to neither of them. Before then, however, she had had three summers in which she could begin to rediscover her true nature.

At six o'clock in the summer, at seven in autumn, I was out of doors, aware of the rain-drenched roses, or the red leaves of the cherry-trees quivering in the red November dawn. The silver-coated rats squatted at ease, eating their meal of grapes straight from the vine; the big snake, caught in the trellis of the hen-run, could not escape the fowls' ferocity. The swallows ruled the cat with extreme rigour, driving it away with sharp blows of their beaks and shrill whistling war-cries from the barn and the rows of nests that lined every rafter. I had a bulldog, Toby-Dog, who lived in a turmoil or swoon of emotion, and a long, luxurious, subtle angora cat, 'Kiki-la-Doucette'. A *pégot* cat - the *pégot* cats of the Franche-Comté are those that follow like dogs - attached herself to me Fond, familiar beasts, infinitely precious. I did not talk to them a great deal, since they were always with me . . .

She bought a *petit duc*, 'a carriage that is something between a fairy chariot and a child's pushcart', and drove it through the lanes, stopping every now and then to gather flowers and fruits, chestnuts and mushrooms. She was, she concluded later, learning to live. 'Can one learn to live? Yes, if you are not happy.'

Here, 'vaguely aware of a duty towards myself, which was to write something other than the *Claudines*', she wrote a book to please herself, one which was not about love. This was the charming *Dialogues des bêtes*, which would win her a new public so devoted and persistent that, even forty years later, admirers seeing her with a bulldog in an Alpine hotel would ask Maurice Goudeket if this was not 'Toby-Dog'. Her devotion to animals was as profound as her respect for them – 'our perfect companions', she was to say, 'never have fewer than four feet'; but no one gave the lie more completely than Colette to the stupid but often-trumpeted notion that a love for pet animals is in itself an expression of incapacity for loving other human beings.

The one flaw of these summers was Willy's occasional descent, for he brought with him the whiff of corruption. He brought also small trunks full of pornography, which he would leave in her care – 'these repulsive volumes are worth a great deal of money' he would say. Her spirits lifted when he hurried back to Paris; yet his departures were still painful for he took with him 'the persistent normal dream: a couple living together in the country'.

Nevertheless these summers, in which she could feel herself becoming another and better person, prepared her for the break with Willy, even though she was to be surprised to discover that he was getting ready to dispense with her himself.

The break came gradually, as inevitable ruptures often do ... The marriage could only have endured if Colette had remained ignorant and submissive. Yet, even as she began to recognize what was going to happen, the prospect was frightening. Marriage was still, for provincial girls, a lifetime career. The Code Napoléon was firm on that point. 'To desert the domestic hearth' was not a light undertaking. The law treated women as minors. If a woman committed adultery, she was liable to imprisonment for a period of between three and twenty-four months. (A husband could indulge in it with impunity, of course, only committing an offence if he actually maintained a concubine in the family home.) Nor was this aspect of the law a dead letter; far from it; the Radical politician Georges Clemenceau (Prime Minister in 1917–18) actually had his wife charged with adultery (though extremely unfaithful himself) when he was Minister of the Interior; she was moreover imprisoned. No wonder Colette hesitated to commit herself. As Nathalie Barney put it, 'In those days people were still afraid to be involved in scandal.'

And yet . . . the immature girl who had married Willy no longer existed. He had introduced her to a world that made light of bourgeois scruples, and disregarded conventional morality. He had shown her too that she had marketable talents, even though she was not yet determined on a career as a writer; indeed she disliked the idea: she had never wanted to write and now it was a craft tainted by its association with her husband.

Her theatrical connections, the friendship she had formed with Marguerite Moreno, Polaire and other actresses, the attraction which amateur theatricals held for many of their acquaintance, pointed an alternative way of escape. For some years Colette had had a gymnasium in her apartment – it was a fashionable fad, and her practice had become well known. She had even appeared on a postcard – postcards of fashionable beauties were a feature of the age in France as in England, where shop-boys had swooned over Lily Langtry

– *Mme Colette Willy et le Culte Physique*. Might she perhaps go on the stage? As a dancer or mime? Willy was encouraging – after all, it was good publicity, and, though Colette did not yet realize it, he too was looking for a way out of the marriage, which had begun – no one knows why – to displease him. She put her toe in the water. The first experience was hardly encouraging. She appeared with an American girl, Eva Palmer, in a sketch written by Pierre Louÿs. Both were overcome by nerves. Miss Palmer stammered; Colette's rolling Burgundian 'r's' made her accent sound 'positively Russian'. The author observed that it had been 'an unforgettable experience to hear my words spoken by Mark Twain and Tolstoy'. Nevertheless, very soon, Willy was offering to send her 'on a little trip' in a play which he called his own. 'Brussels,' he suggested, 'is always interested in certain forms of entertainment, in well-known people . . .' Besides, such an undertaking would 'provide an excellent opportunity of getting rid of this wearisome flat and of finding an adequate arrangement suited to a different form of life . . .'

It took her a little while to realize this was the sack.

It was a mistake on Willy's part. He was never able to repeat the success of Colette-Claudine . . . He continued as a literary capitalist, but less and less successfully; perhaps there were by now too many graduates from his school for him to be able to carry on the bluff, maintain the pretence of his own authorship. As one, Ernest La Jeunesse, said, 'I did what everyone else has done – I began by calling myself Willy.' But when they outgrew that stage, editors found

Willy superfluous. A residue of bitterness can be seen in Colette's story in *Le Képi* of a woman who was writing a Hindu novel at one sou a line. 'Why one sou?' 'Because she was working for a fellow who got two, who was working for someone who got four, who was working for another who got ten . . .' As for Willy: with his second wife, Meg Villars, he had another shot at Claudine with a novel, *Les Imprudences de Peggy*; then, with his third wife, Madeleine de Evrante, tried it again, with *Mady écolière*. Neither Peggy nor Mady was a Claudine; perhaps Willy had simply outlived the period to which he had belonged. Like many whose talents are second-rate, he depended on his ability to catch the flavour of the moment. Colette, however, was to prove herself less ephemeral.

CHAPTER THREE

Lesbos

Colette and Willy separated in May 1905, though divorce proceedings did not begin for another eighteen months and their divorce did not become final till 1910. Colette established herself, with Toby-Dog and the cat Kiki-la-Doucette, in a ground-floor apartment in the Rue de Villejust. It was not distinguished; no one of any standing lived at street level; but her independent life had begun in poverty, and indeed she would hardly know financial security till her last years.

She was not to marry again till 1913. In the interval her way of life became extraordinary in comparison even with what it had been before, and was to be subsequently. These years, and the years of her second marriage, completed her education and development. After her second divorce, the pattern was made; the writer had acquired her subject matter and thereafter all her work was retrospective.

Anita Brookner has summed up those years after Willy. She became 'a lesbian, a transvestite, a music-hall performer of dubious quality, a chronicler of opium addiction and homosexual love affairs . . . This hard-headed hard-working ardent and humiliated woman created the stereotype woman who presides over her own emotional life, and who appeals to those who desire to do the same.' Colette's woman is not a victim, differing in this from the heroines in Jean Rhys's novels whom she might be thought to resemble; Colette was too tough, too much her mother's daughter, to permit self-pity.

She was not fully committed to being a writer in 1905. Writing was associated with Willy; it was the sentence to which he had condemned her. Moreover, as the breach between them gradually widened she found herself cut off from literary Montmartre. She had anyway little reputation as a writer, since Willy had annexed the *Claudines*. However, she was able very gradually to strengthen her position. When the *Claudines* appeared in a new edition the author was named as Colette-Willy. She managed to re-work the two *Minne* books (successors to *Claudine*), and when they came out as *L'Ingénue libertine* in 1909 to revise them sufficiently so that she could write to Lucien Solvay: 'During the days when Willy did me the dubious honour of signing my novels, he would often insert in them phrases designed to satisfy his personal grudges. He called this collaborating – my first concern has been to remove these unfortunate epithets,' including a malicious caricature of Solvay.

Nevertheless the establishment of herself as a writer was a slow and reluctant process. She sought other means of supporting herself, and turned to the theatre and music-hall; it was a world which appealed to her bruised and damaged spirit. Its freemasonry was comforting. Discipline, which she always valued, was required, but judgement came free of morality, and censure was reserved for those who did not do their job properly. Between 1906 and 1912 she spent part of every year on tour, either in dance or mime, or playing Claudine herself or taking part in a hugely successful and frequently revived melodrama, *La Chair* (*The Flesh*). There was disagreement about her talent, but she won high marks for discipline and professionalism.

At the same time she entered the world of Gomorrah, moving with cautious curiosity. She was attracted by all in it that was maternal and sisterly, seemly and gentle. She found it far removed from Willy's corrupt grossness and salacity; she admired the taste and reticence of its inhabitants and found them soothing. She was touched by the realization that

among these women, free yet timorous, addicted to late hours, darkened rooms, gambling and indolence, I never detected a trace of cynicism. Sparing of words, all they needed was an allusion. I heard one of them – one only – a German princess with the fresh chubby face of a butcher boy – introduce her *petite amie* one day as 'my spouse', whereupon my blunt gentlemen in skirts wrinkled their noses in distaste and pretended not to hear. 'It's not that I conceal anything,' briefly commented the Vicomtesse de X, 'it's simply that I don't like showing off.'

With such women she could be a daughter again, but without the constraints imposed by a real mother; she felt less obligation to pretend to happiness.

Sido was at first dismayed by the change in Colette's life. Though she had never cared for Willy, she now wrote to ask whether he could not forbid his wife to appear on the stage. 'Have you no authority?' she asked. 'It's scandalous.' This outburst was occasioned by Colette's appearance in a mime with the Marquise de Belboeuf, itself a remarkable story.

The Marquise de Belboeuf was among the most striking of the inhabitants of Gomorrah. She was the daughter of the Duc de Morny, a bastard half-brother of Napoleon III, whom he had served as Foreign Minister. She belonged therefore to the Napoleonic aristocracy, always on the raffish side compared to the old nobility of pre-Revolutionary France. The Princesse Marie de Morny, known generally as 'Missy', a pet name given to her by a governess, had been married, when very young, to the Marquis de Belboeuf. It did not take; it offended her nature. They soon separated, and thereafter Missy dressed as a man and had her servants address her as 'Monsieur le Marquis'. She was over forty when Colette came to know her, and decidedly odd-looking. Her features were fine, but, to disguise the femininity of her figure, she wore an assortment of shirts and woollen waistcoats that made her look a bit like a teddy bear. Her feet were very small and so she wore several pairs of socks to fill up her man's shoes. In later life out of a residual sense of propriety she once wore a dress when attending her brother's funeral. This disturbed her nephews and nieces, who thought 'she looked like a man dressed up as a woman' and begged her to go and change. She was shy, sentimental and fundamentally insecure. It would be hard to find a greater contrast to Willy than this timid and loving aristocrat. Willy of course found her a great joke; it amused him to travel in railway-carriages reserved for ladies, and, when challenged, reply, 'But I am the Marquise de Belboeuf.'

Missy had written a pantomime, *Le Rêve d'Égypte*, and nothing would do but that she and Colette should appear in it together at the Moulin Rouge: the posters proclaimed *Yssim: and Colette Willy*, and all Paris was stirred up. The Morny family were furious and filled the house with hired thugs. Willy and his new mistress Meg Villars appeared prominently in a box ... When Colette and Missy, Colette scantily clad in gauze drapes, closed in a long and passionate embrace, pandemonium broke out in the theatre. Willy stood up and bowed, was booed and attacked. The scandal was much relished, François Pascal writing in *L'Éclair de Montpellier*: 'The pantomime could just as well have been a reproduction of scenes from the private life of the three persons involved in it and it presented a spectacle of such audacious immorality that the entire audience rose against them.' The police forbade further performances and closed the theatre. Willy had reached that point of self-infatuation when any sort of notoriety offers the keenest pleasure; he said smugly that, having received a telegram warning him not to attend, he had naturally gone. Meg Villars wrote to his son Jacques that 'I applauded ... not because I think Colette is a good actress (she isn't) and the Marquise is just awful, but I enjoyed showing that I wasn't afraid of them.' However, even for Willy, the consequences were bitter: he lost his job on *L'Écho de Paris*. Two weeks later he filed for divorce (Colette laid a countersuit alleging infidelity). From this point his bitterness against Colette, and his wish to hurt her, grew. It would not be long before he was commissioning a novel and instructing his *nègre* that he wanted a certain character 'to resemble – blatantly – Mme Colette Willy, both physically and in her predilections'.

As for Colette, she had made a fool of herself; she had to endure cruel criticism and a cartoon called *Claudine en ménage*, showing her in scanty Egyptian costume in the arms of a top-hatted, riding-coated Missy. She had certainly burned her boats with this public display, and perhaps that had been her intention. Yet it was curious; she disliked notoriety; Willy had damaged her self-confidence and her sense of her own being, and what she sought from Missy was primarily a renewal of her health. In Anthony Powell's *A Dance to the Music of Time*, General Conyers suggests that what happens to someone does not necessarily matter if his personal myth remains intact; Colette may be seen in the years after Willy to be reconstructing her personal myth, making herself into a person with whom she could live comfortably.

She lived with Missy for the best part of six years. Sometimes they shared a house, sometimes not. Sometimes Missy accompanied her on tour. Colette drew strength and comfort from her: 'Profiting from Missy's presence,' she wrote in 1908 to her friend Léon Hamel, 'I have treated myself to a fine case of flu . . .' Missy was ever ready to cosset her, acting as a stay in Colette's erratic life. They were lovers, but Missy was also an alternative mother, and Colette took pleasure in being a daughter again. To please Missy, and perhaps herself, Colette dressed as a boy or young man, though she said later, 'I was not long deluded by these photographs which show me wearing a stiff mannish collar, necktie, short jacket over a skirt' (or, more frequently, trousers), 'a lighted cigarette between my fingers ...' Perhaps not; she was playing a part, like Sebastian Flyte in *Brideshead Revisited* when he used to dine at the George in false whiskers, 'playing at tigers', as Anthony Blanche put it in that novel. Yet the play was serious enough, even though the painter Boldini penetrated her disguise: 'You're the one who goes on stage without tights?' he asked. 'And who dances – *così, così* – quite naked?' Colette denied it indignantly. 'He was not even listening. He laughed shrewdly, insinuatingly, and patted my cheek. "My, what a proper young lady we are," he murmured, "what a proper young lady we are." ' It could hardly be gainsaid. She was still Sido's daughter. As another observer, a newspaper interviewer, put it, years later: 'Madame Colette is a bourgeoise, an authentic bourgeoise. Even in a hotel she has to "dress up" her room.'

Colette had however formed the habits of a writer, though she neither realized nor yet accepted this fact. There was from now on a part of herself which stood off and observed her own actions. Everything that she did, everything that happened to her, became 'material' and would be used, transmuted into art. (She is indeed among the most personal of writers.) It is in general this fact, more than any other, which separates the writer from the world and society wherein he or she moves: life is copy, imperfect and never fully realized, till re-shaped and interpreted in written words, a statement not contradicted by the intensity with which Colette lived, by the close scrutiny she gave to all manifestations of the natural world. So now, though Colette did not enter the Tout-Paris of Gomorrah in search of material, for something in the life of these women satisfied the demands of her nature and it was a necessary experiment, yet she could never fully belong to that world, not only because she was truly bisexual, never ceasing to love and desire a man, but also because, for her, experience had already become insufficient in itself; it must be re-ordered in prose. In much the same way, an alcoholic writer like Malcolm Lowry is never simply a man who drinks too much and is destroying himself; there is always a creative artist standing at an oblique angle to the man's experience and waiting to write *Under the Volcano*. To put it another way, Willy, by forcing Colette to be a writer, had made it impossible for her to live with full spontaneity.

It would be a long time before she would write of her experiences of lesbian love; that she would write of them was soon evident to her, but they required a slow maturation, and *Ces plaisirs* was not published till 1932, a quarter of a century after she had appeared on stage with Missy. That she had had the intention earlier is shown by what she wrote to Proust when *Sodome et Gomorrhe* appeared: 'No one in the world has written such pages on inversion, but no one. Years ago I wanted to write a study of sexual inversion myself, and it was the substance of your pages that I wanted to express. But my laziness or incapacity failed to get them down . . .'

This was disingenuous, if only because Colette's view of homosexual love was gentler and less despairing than Proust's; yet her admiration for what he had done was sincere: she saw that he had made it possible to write about this subject without moral indignation or innuendo, without regarding homosexuals as 'cases'. He had shown homosexuality to be a natural condition.

For Colette it was not only that, but one in which it was possible for a woman to be tender and loving, and tenderly loved. In some ways, the most interesting and revealing chapter of *Ces plaisirs* is the seventh. All the rest of the book contains elements of autobiography. This chapter tells the story, surely new to most French readers, of the Ladies of Llangollen, 'two well-born young girls related to the Welsh aristocracy, who, in May 1778, ran away together and, having chosen their fate, cloistered their solitude, their reciprocal tenderness, for fifty-three years . . .' 'Their reciprocal tenderness': it was this feature which attracted and moved Colette. She could never, she said, 'sufficiently blame the Sapphos met by chance in restaurants, in dance halls, on the Blue Train, on the pavement, those provocative women who laugh but cannot sigh'. There should be nothing of libertinage in lesbian love. Instead, she looked admiringly on the delight experienced by the Ladies of Llangollen and recorded by Lady Eleanor Butler in her diary: 'a day of delicious and exquisite retirement'. 'In living amorously together,' Colette suggests,

two women may discover that their mutual attraction is not basically sensual ... what woman would not blush to seek out her *amie* only for sensual pleasure? In no way is it passion that fosters the devotion of two women, but rather a feeling of kinship ...

... perhaps this love which according to some people is outrageous, escapes the changing seasons and the wanings of love by being controlled with invisible severity, nourished on very little, permitted to live gropingly and without a goal, its unique flower being a mutual trust such as that other love can never plumb or comprehend, but only envy; and so great is such a love that by its grace a half century can pass by like a day of 'exquisite and delicious retirement'.

For Lady Eleanor Butler and Miss Sarah Ponsonby, yes; but not for Colette and Missy. No doubt Colette, only just beginning to be aware of her extraordinary abilities, was not ready for such retirement; no doubt too Missy, confused and exigent, insecure and snobbish, half-man, half-woman, was incapable of the repose, the self-assurance, at once undemanding and profoundly demanding, which Lady Eleanor Butler had manifested. This chapter is however in a way a tribute to Missy; it tenderly and sadly suggests what might have been; it holds out an ideal relationship, of which Colette's and Missy's had been no more than the shadowy representation. For Missy herself appears in *Ces plaisirs*,

scarcely disguised as 'La Chevalière', and she is seen search-
ing 'with her anxious eyes . . . for what she never found: a
settled and sentimental attachment'. Far from finding it,
'this woman with the bearing of a handsome boy endured
the pride and punishment of never being able to establish a
real lasting affair with a woman . . . "I do not know anything
about completeness in love," she cried, "except the idea I
have of it . . ." '

Colette included herself in Missy's list of failures; yet she
also responded quiveringly to her:

The seduction emanating from a being of uncertain or dis-
simulated sex is powerful. Those who have never experienced it
liken it to the banal attraction of the love that evicts the male
element. This is a gross misconception. Anxious and veiled, never
exposed to the light of day, the androgynous creature wanders,
wonders and implores in a whisper . . . There especially remains
for the androgynous creature the right, even the obligation, never
to be happy . . .

This androgynous creature was a stereotype of the *belle
époque*, arising perhaps in reaction to the female self-
consciousness of the New Woman of the 1880s, though the
effeminate seducer and the Dandy as Man-Woman had
featured often in nineteenth-century fiction; Wilde plays
with the idea in *The Importance of Being Earnest*, where the
men are the weaker sex and Gwendolen says, 'Certainly
once a man begins to neglect his domestic duties he becomes
painfully effeminate. And I don't like that. It makes men so
very attractive.' Beardsley's art belongs to the androgynous

world and fascinated Colette. In an undated letter to Robert de Montesquieu, the poet-aesthete who was one of the originals for Proust's Charlus, she wrote:

At least three times I have read your study of Beardsley for whom I have an almost guilty passion. The drawings of this very young and rather mad young man correspond so closely to what is hidden in me. I have so longed to live, if only for an hour, in front of that garlanded dressing-table, whose mirror would reflect behind my shoulder the black velvet mask of the creature in disguise: the creature who has such pointed fingers . . .

The androgyne, and the concept of androgyny, would be central to her art, where the women so often have the traditional masculine strengths (in *Chéri* she talks of Léa's 'virility') and the men a delicacy and languor, a weakness of will, historically attributed to women. In all her fiction the sexes blur in a sensuous glow, losing their conventional attributes, and this is true even when the characters she creates have no conscious orientation towards their own sex. In that little masterpiece *La Chatte* (*The Cat*, published in 1933) the girl Camille has all the energy and all the power of decision; her husband Alain is passive, refined, in love with his childhood and his Russian Blue cat Saha; his is that delicate moral sensibility, those fine nerves, which in earlier fiction would have belonged to the girl. Here she is brash and insensitive; but it is Alain who is crueller in the end and Alain who has his way. Chéri himself, her most famous creation in her most famous novel, is defined by his passivity and beauty, but even these qualities (for great beauty is a quality) have been created by the women who surround and dominate him. All his revolts are small and petulant, all the decisions in his life are taken by the women; his only autonomous act is his suicide. It is Colette's ability to transcend the sexual barrier and fuse the sexes which is so remarkable. Kay Dick has written, 'I could prove, had I space enough to spare, that Colette is both Léa and Chéri'; in a sense other, evidently, than that she has created both of them. In another gem of a novella, *Bella-Vista*, the central character in a small *pension* in the South of France is a mannish woman called Miss Ruby, the lover of the elderly lady who keeps the *pension*. Miss Ruby seduces a serving girl, and is then revealed to be in fact a man. But fact is perhaps the wrong word here, where everything is precise, yet the differentiation of the sexes is so blurred as to seem unreal . . .

Missy, unhappily wandering in the Waste Land where the sexes meet, resembled Proust's Charlus. Both were drawn to extremes, into what the world sees as absurdity and vice, because both were truly Platonic, in search of the perfect union of souls and bodies. Neither was capable of settling for less, as are those who turn to promiscuity; neither was prepared to compromise. Both wanted to be mother, father, brother, sister, husband, wife, lover, child, to one other person, filling all roles at the same time. Colette saw this, and saw the tragedy, that the demands made were so extreme as to be unattainable; yet she saw also the nobility of the attempt, and her realization of the tragedy was perhaps truer than Proust's because she had less for which to forgive herself.

Her sojourn in Lesbos refined her understanding of human nature and deepened her capacity for pity. There was the Anglo-American girl, Pauline Tarn, beautiful, neurotic, a poet who called herself Renée Vivien, who lived on a little fruit, alcohol, opium, by the Bois de Boulogne across two garden courts from Colette's apartment in the Rue de Villejust. Colette admired her, loved her and was wary of her impulse to self-destruction. Renée Vivien had a demanding lover, a great woman, who would 'requisition her at a moment's notice', and who would, she told Colette, one day 'kill her'. 'In four words she explained how she might perish. Four words of a frankness to make you blink. This would not be worth telling, except for what Renée said then: "With her I dare not lie or pretend, because at that moment she lays her ear over my heart." And a little later she did die, starving herself, sipping alcohol.' Colette, remaining tender, still bridled: 'Like all those who never use their strength to the limit, I am hostile to those who let life burn them out.' Colette retained a provincial sense of the moral value of reserve: 'Two habits have enabled me to restrain my tears,' she wrote once, 'that of concealing my thoughts, and that of using mascara on my eyelashes ...' Nor could she really sympathize with those who deny themselves food. Colette was always greedy; her letters are stuffed with descriptions of meals, and she regarded a good dinner as the best cure for a sad heart, once taking a friend, whose mother had just died, to Prunier's to eat prawns to console her.

There was more wisdom to be found from Amalia, an old

actress with a touring company, who was able to say, 'I had everything, beauty, happiness, misery, men and women . . . you can call it a life . . .' It was Amalia too who told her: 'Get this into your head – a couple of women can live together a long time and be happy. But if one of the two women lets herself behave in the slightest like a pseudo-man, then . . .' 'Then the couple become unhappy?' 'Not necessarily unhappy, but sad . . . you see, when a woman remains a woman, she is a complete human being. She lacks nothing even insofar as her *amie* is concerned. But if she ever gets it into her head to try to be a man, she's grotesque . . .'

To illustrate this, she told the story of a woman known as La Lucienne. This woman, a contemporary of hers, had been filled with an insatiable desire to dominate. She loved breaking up marriages, carrying off the wife and then discarding her. As the years passed her obsession with playing the part of a dashing man-about-town, a ladykiller, a *roué*, grew upon her. 'If her lady friends sometimes forgot that she wasn't a man, she, for her part, never stopped thinking about it.' It made her discontented and cruel. She played all the mean tricks of the love affair, as if (though Colette doesn't say so) she had modelled herself on Valmont in *Les Liaisons dangereuses*.

One night she threw her lover, a pretty blonde called Loulou, half-naked out into the garden, in order to punish her and compel her to choose between her and her husband. Before dawn, she leaned out and put the question to her. The girl said she was going back to her husband. 'I've just realized he can do something you can't.' 'Oh naturally,' says Lucienne spitefully ... 'No,' says Loulou, 'it's not what you think. I'm not all that crazy about you know what. But I'm going to tell you something. When you and I go out together, everyone takes you for a man, that's understood. But for my part, I feel humiliated to be with a man who can't do *pipi* against a wall ...'

For Amalia, Loulou had found 'the unkindest thing in the world to say ...'

For the sake of her art, Colette pretended not to understand. But she understood well enough, and so gave the story prominence.

These were years of continuing education. Later, when she was embarking on *Ces plaisirs*, she wrote to Marguerite Moreno: 'I'm writing something about unisexuals – frightful word. Obviously one could treat the subject in one sentence: "There are no unisexuals." ' Sido's daughter could not help but respond to the tenderness she found in this world; yet, like the Cat she played on stage and indeed physically resembled, she declined to commit herself fully to it.

She was alive to its attraction and its uncertainties. Yet she said that Proust was mistaken in assembling 'a Gomorrah of inscrutable and depraved young girls'; because

there is no such thing as Gomorrah. Puberty, boarding schools, solitude, prisons, aberrations, snobbishness – they are all seed-beds, but too shallow to engender and sustain a vice that could attract a great number or become an established thing that would gain the indispensable solidarity of its votaries. Intact, enormous, eternal, Sodom looks down from its heights upon its puny counterfeit . . .

What did she mean by this? It is a verdict which will offend some modern readers, and indeed it has to be read within the context of Colette's own times. France was, as I have said, a patriarchal society. The Code Napoléon made wives and daughters utterly subordinate to husbands and fathers. Few reputable careers were open to women – they might work in factories and shops of course, in restaurants and music-halls and in the theatre; they could go on the streets. They could teach in girls' schools and they could write books; little else. True, almost 40 per cent of Frenchwomen worked; but these almost all belonged to the lower classes. As for property, though marriage normally involved community of property, and marriage settlements were often devised so as to protect a bride's share of her own family property, the law did not provide for community in its management; that was the husband's prerogative. Women's position was in some ways ambiguous. The English feminist Violet Stuart-Wortley considered that 'though legally women occupy a much inferior status to men, in practice they constitute the superior sex. They are the "power behind the throne" and in business relations undoubtedly enjoy greater consideration than English-women'; yet this was a personal impression, just as any power enjoyed by a woman depended on her personal qualities. It was not hers by right. She was excluded of course from public life, not even having the vote till 1945. Theodore Zeldin observes that 'the simultaneous idealization and repression of women was one of the ways by which French society developed its peculiar characteristics'.

No wonder then that the inhabitants of Gomorrah could not rival those of Sodom in self-confidence. In a man's world, they were always tempted to become imitation-men, and to become so in no spirit of parody (such as was always present among those men who preferred to wear female garb; who were in any effect withdrawing from the social struggle, not challenging it). For men to live without women was natural enough; for women to dispense with men, and yet remain in the world, was a revolutionary act.

Colette recognized this gallantry in her lesbian lovers, friends and acquaintances. She saw in them an expression of the ideals of the French Revolution which had been denied to their sex. They asserted their right to Liberty and Equality, and, if they could find no grand word to put in the place of Fraternity (for Sorority, its apparent equivalent, does not represent a condition as fraternity does), they nevertheless sought that female equivalent. They were refugees from a world made by, and for, men; and, if, in their flight and challenge, many found themselves aping the men they had rejected, that was hardly surprising. They retained all of them, in her eyes, a certain timidity. It could hardly be otherwise. Those whom she most frequented, because of her affair with Missy, constituted a society perishing on the margin of society ... Their snobbishness undermined their rebellion. They tried, trembling with fear, to live without hypocrisy, the breathable air of society. This clique, or sect, claimed the right of 'personal freedom' and equality with homosexuality, that imperturbable establishment. And they scoffed, if in whispers, at Papa Lepine, the Prefect of Police, who never could take lightly the question of women in men's clothes.

For which reason they would shroud themselves in a heavy all-concealing cloak when passing from their carriage to their rendezvous ... Their lovers were often working-class girls, because, Colette explains, most of them had been brought up principally by servants, among whom they experienced a freedom and sense of equality they sought to recapture: 'They found again the tremulous and secret pleasure of their childhood when dining at the servants' table.' They were, too, 'almost as fond of the horse, that warm, enigmatic, stubborn and sensitive creature, as they were of their young protégées . . .'

They might seem a little absurd. Colette, aware of their sensitive, deprived, yet ever optimistic natures, did not find them so. She revelled indeed 'in the admirable quickness of their half-spoken language, the exchange of threats, of promises, as if, once the slow-thinking male had been banished, every message from woman to woman became clear and overwhelming restricted to a small but infallible number of signs'.

They did much for her. They healed the bruises which were Willy's legacy. She learned much about her own sex, and what she learned went to deepen and enrich her writing. Her years with Missy, years also when she made her living in the theatres and music-halls, restored her self-confidence, reminded her that she was desirable.

CHAPTER FOUR

Sidi and Sido's Death

In these years, despite experiencing 'the very common crisis of being broke', Colette learned she could live on her own, as a free woman, and support herself. She never set up permanent house with Missy, originally for fear of scandal, then because she wished to guard her independence. They were often together, on tour, or in Paris where they would eat at a little restaurant called Palmyre's in the Place Blanche whose proprietrix, Colette told Hamel, 'smothers us with maternal care, cooks little steaks for Missy and yesterday had us inspect the three pups her bulldog Bellotte had just whelped'; they took holidays in the country and in the autumn of 1909 made a trip to Brittany in search of a villa, eventually finding one at Rozven, near Saint-Malo. All the same, simply because Colette was busy in the theatre and the music-hall, because she was also working hard as a writer, having accepted, however reluctantly, that this was her *métier*, and so forging her mastery of her craft, she and Missy could never find themselves equivalents of the Ladies of Llangollen, though such a life may well have been Missy's desire; not for them, though, years passed in 'a delicious and exquisite retirement'.

These years in the music-halls, where her companions were mostly working-class boys and girls, men and women, struggling for security in a precarious environment, gave Colette a respect for the virtues of industry and professionalism which was to last all her life; they strengthened her core of provincial good sense; they brought her up against the hard facts of economic reality. When she began to write about them, in music-hall sketches which appeared in *Le Matin* at irregular intervals from December 1910 and were to be published in book form as *L'Envers du music-hall* in 1913, she paid tribute to their humour, their resilience, their fortitude in the face of misfortune. She drew strength from them, learning before he uttered it the truth of Hemingway's expression of faith: 'Man can be defeated but not destroyed.' It was in the same spirit that she was to say of herself years later, 'I have very often deprived myself of the necessities of life, but I have never consented to give up a luxury.'

In the autumn after that trip to Brittany with Missy she began to write her first piece of mature fiction. *La Vagabonde* was to be serialized in *La Vie Parisienne* from May 1910; that autumn it got three votes in the first round of voting for the Prix Goncourt, the literary prize which carried the greatest prestige. *La Vagabonde*, though old-fashioned in being written in epistolary form, is nevertheless truly modern in the emphasis it lays on female sexuality and work. It suffers, like its successor, *L'Entrave* (*The Fetter*, but translated into

English as *The Captive*), from being written too close to the personal experience from which it is drawn – Taillandy in *La Vagabonde* is an obvious portrait of Willy, and all the characters and the central situation in *L'Entrave* can be too exactly identified. Colette recognized this herself; when she finished *L'Entrave* she wrote of it with more than the distaste normal to an author on completing a novel and finding it inferior to its original ideal conception: 'I rejoice in the relief, but I vomit on it. I despise it.' Nevertheless both novels marked a new maturity and seriousness, and *La Vagabonde* has been named among the twelve best French novels of the century, though it seems to me markedly inferior to the *Chéri* books or to *Julie de Corneilhan*.

In 1910 Colette encountered a young man, Auguste Hériot, who fell in love with her. They met at Polaire's – Hériot had been her lover. He was rich – his family owned the department store the Grands Magasins du Louvre – handsome and agreeable. When Colette's divorce from Willy became final, he proposed marriage. Missy was not jealous. She liked and approved of Hériot, and, to the extent that her love for Colette was also maternal, saw him as an ideal son-in-law. Colette told Hamel that 'Missy basically adores Hériot. She had even prepared him a room here at Rozven and she intended to impose him on me quasi-conjugally. That's all I need to disgust me with this young man for ever,' she added.

The marriage would have been 'sensible'. Hériot could support her, give her freedom to write. He would have respected her identity and her need for liberty. His devotion

77

was unquestioned. Sido approved of him. But Colette stopped short; it would have been for her a marriage of convenience. In January and February 1911 she was in Nice with Hériot and a young actress, Lily de Remé: at first she glowed: 'These two infants, both in love with me ... my own ego derives maternal satisfaction from their appetite and fresh complexions,' she told Hamel. But maternal satisfaction was not enough; she had already met Henri de Jouvenel. In April 1911 she was writing to the novelist Louis de Robert: 'I'm finally emerging from my "vulgarity crisis". Sated I have left the fake Midi and my companions' (who by this time included Missy). Colette had fallen in love and was ready to throw her hard-won freedom and independence overboard, and, like Renée, the heroine of *L'Entrave*, return to the cage, even though she recognized the bars through which she had previously slipped.

Henri de Jouvenel represented a new temptation and an old danger. His birth, character and history all proclaimed him to be a masterful man. He belonged to an old family of Limousin barons. His full name was de Jouvenel des Ursins, and he proudly claimed a connection with the great Roman family, the Orsini. The family had been noble since the fourteenth century. They had embraced Protestantism in the sixteenth and declined after the revocation of the Edict of Nantes, in 1687, before being restored to prosperity in the nineteenth century by Léon de Jouvenel, who had married a relation of President Casimir-Périer. Henri was born in 1876, so he was three years younger than Colette. He was educated at the Collège Stanislaus and the École

Normale Supérieure, and, being unable to live off the rents of his properties, had become a journalist, being appointed editor of *Le Matin* in 1902. The same year he married Claire Boas, the daughter of the newspaper's proprietor. His new father-in-law was Jewish, but de Jouvenel, with the careless arrogance of the aristocratic socialist, was happy to ignore the conventional prejudices of his class. They had one son, Bertrand, born in 1903, but the marriage did not last and was dissolved three years later.

De Jouvenel was a ladies' man and a duellist, of forceful personality and great energy. When he met Colette he had been for some years the lover of a fellow aristocrat, Isabelle de Comminges, a woman of spectacular beauty known as *La Panthère* (the Panther). The Panther learned of his new interest and Colette found herself embroiled in a drama which had all the staple ingredients of the hammiest romantic fiction.

On 31 July 1911 she wrote to Hamel telling him that the Panther now knew what was happening:

Upon which she declared that she would kill this woman, no matter who. Desperate, Jouvenel transmitted this threat, upon which I replied 'I'm going to see her.' And I went. And I told the Panther, 'I'm the woman.' Upon which she melted and entreated me. But her contrition was short-lived for two days later she announced to J. her threat to knife me. Desperate again, J. had me picked up by Sauerwein [an editor at *Le Matin*] in a car, and, still with Sauerwein, accompanied me to Rozven. Here we found Missy glacial and disgusted, having just received news of what was happening from the Panther. Then my two guardians left me, and

79

Paul Barlet mounted guard, with a revolver, no less. Missy, still glacial and disgusted, flew the coop and went to Honfleur. Three days later, J. summoned me back to his side by telephone and Sauerwein came to pick me up by car, because the Panther was out on the prowl, looking for me and armed with a revolver. Here began my period of semi-sequestration in Paris, where I was guarded like a precious reliquary by the Sûreté as well as by Jouvenel, Sauerwein and Sapène, three pillars of *Le Matin*. And believe it or not, this period has come to an end, thanks to an unexpected providential and magnificent event. Tired of waiting around, M. Hériot and – if you please – Mme La Panthère – no less – have just embarked on his yacht for a six week cruise, after having astonished Le Havre, their home port, with their drunken orgies. Is that good? Is it good theatre? Just a little too much, wouldn't you say? Meantime Jouvenel has distinguished himself by very proper behaviour which earned him the displeasure of Missy . . .

Beneath the humour, one can catch a note of an almost schoolgirlish excitement. She had indeed plunged into love: Jouvenel is 'tender, jealous, unsociable and incurably honest', she assured Hamel, even though she recognized his womanizing tendencies sufficiently clearly to nickname him 'Sidi' or 'the pasha'. But at the moment it did not matter. She had received the *coup de foudre*. On 25 August she wrote to André Rouveyre, 'You will not see Missy with me again, my friend. We are no longer living together.' A few days later, writing to Christiane Mendelys, she was arch in her revelation: 'But who told you I have been neglecting physical culture? I just have a new method, that's all. The Sidi Method. It's excellent. But no public courses . . . private

Colette as a child

Captain Colette and
Sido in the garden
'down there'

" 'I'll be a sailor' ... because she often dreamed of being a boy ..." (*My Mother's House*)

Claudine covers; Polaire, Willy, Colette

Willy with Toby-Dog

Colette as a
man-about-town

The music-hall
performer

Colette and Missy

The woman of fashion
and her bulldogs

With 'that cat'

Above, left: Henri de Jouvenal
Above, right: Bertrand de Jouvenal

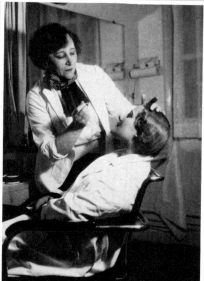

The beauty salon, at work on her daughter Bel-Gazou

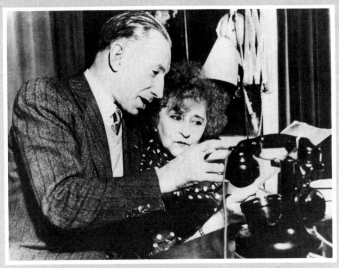

With Maurice Goudeket

Old age: 'the raft'

The schoolgirl

The young wife

The writer

The sage

lessons only . . . extremely private . . . News of Missy? I have none, and she continues to detain my belongings . . .' In this new excitement even Sido, the beloved mother, could seem an encumbrance. Between these two letters she also wrote to her old music-hall partner, Georges Wague: 'I can tell you at least that I am leaving for Châtillon . . . where my blessed mother is being extremely difficult, not that she's seriously ill, but she has an attack of "I want to see my daughter". Sidi has allowed me a maximum of three days . . .' Nothing shows more clearly how Sidi had overwhelmed her, deprived her of the independence she had fought so hard to achieve: 'Sidi has allowed me a maximum of three days' to visit Sido; 'an attack of "I want to see my daughter" '; at no other period of her life could Colette have dismissed her mother's wishes in words that do not escape having a ring of contempt.

Like Willy, Sidi at once involved Colette in his own life, hiring her to write a column in *Le Matin*. He faced opposition, for despite the three votes *La Vagabonde* had won in the Prix Goncourt, Colette's reputation was poor. The assistant editor Stéphane Lauzanne threatened to leave if Jouvenel took on 'that tumbler'. As Sidi's second son, Renaud, the child of his liaison with the Panther, put it later: 'Everyone was well aware, much more so than anyone is today, that she had been one of those half-naked dancing-girls whose naughty photographs are still preserved in certain albums.' However, Sidi's will prevailed; Colette became a journalist, with a regular column, *One Thousand and One Nights*, which first appeared anonymously, but was soon signed Colette Willy.

Sido disapproved of this development. 'Minet-Chérie,' she wrote in October, 'you'll be writing a weekly column for *Le Matin*. That's a lot of work and I don't approve because journalism is death to the novelist. It's a pity you're doing it. Protect your talent, my darling, be sparing of it, it's worth the trouble . . .'

The advice was good, but Colette's talent was strong and distinctive enough to survive. For one thing she never lost her personal voice in her journalism, which soon indeed became exceedingly varied, for *Le Matin* began to use her as a special reporter too. Lauzanne's objections were overcome; he realized that though Colette had no experience of journalism and would indeed always proclaim her dislike of writing to a deadline, she had a quite unusual ability. In the next few years she reported flights of dirigibles and balloons, criminal trials (including that of the French Bluebeard Landru), general elections, and, when war came, reported from the front. She also did drama criticism and wrote about cowboy films. After the war she became the paper's literary editor. Like Hemingway, she learned from her experience of newspaper work. In a preface to her friend Renée Hamon's book *Aux Îles de Lumière*, she summed up what she had learned from the trade. Replying to the imaginary problem a beginner might pose, 'But I don't know what to put in a book,' she says:

Neither do I, if you can believe it. I've merely got a few little ideas about what's better left out. Paint nothing that you have not seen. Look for a long time at what pleases you, and longer still at what pains you. Try to be faithful to your first impression. Have no faith in the 'rare word'. Don't wear yourself out by lying. A lie develops imagination and imagination is death to the reporter. Take notes . . . no, don't take notes. Beware of 'flourishes', beware of rushing into poetry. Don't write your report when you are where the event is happening, or it will seem unrecognizable to you when you come back here. One doesn't write a love story while one is making love . . .

Yet, in one way, it seemed as if Sido might be right. There was no fiction between *L'Entrave* in 1913 and *Mitsou* in 1919; but then those were the war years.

Sido had couched her objections in terms of literary criticism: 'I preferred, yes really, I preferred the other one,' she said. 'But, Maman, he was an imbecile.' 'Yes, but you would write beautiful things married to the imbecile.' No doubt she was sincere in this; she had always taken a passionate interest in her daughter's writing. Yet her concern had another basis; she distrusted the type of man she discerned Jouvenel as being; he was likely to make her Minet-Chérie unhappy; and 'You'll spend your time giving him all your most precious gifts.'

For his part, de Jouvenel was ready to ingratiate himself with Sido. He wrote inviting her to come to stay with them. She accepted his invitation

for several reasons, among them one I can never resist: seeing my dear daughter's face and hearing her voice. And then to get to know you and to try to find out why she so enthusiastically threw caution to the winds for your sake. As for me, I shall abandon for a few days the things that rely on me – my cat Mine, who gives me all her trust and tenderness, a sedum that is ready to bloom and is magnificent, a gloxinia whose gaping chalice enables me to watch it seeding at my leisure . . .

But when, years later, Colette wrote one of the most personal of her many personal books, *La Naissance du jour* (*Break of Day*), she transformed this letter of acceptance into a refusal and had Sido give as her reason for declining the invitation the fact that her pink cactus, which only blossomed once every four years, was about to come into flower. It is unlikely that she did not do this deliberately, to emphasize Sido's refined sensibility and contrast it, in her own mind at least, with what she had come by that time to think of as her lover's vulgar blandishments . . . 'We cannot paint a beloved face without passionately distorting it,' she would write in *Mes apprentissages*, but such distortion was done in the name of artistic truth.

There was, however, another reason, less creditable though understandable. Colette felt a guilt and shame usually foreign to her on account of her behaviour in the late summer of 1912. For, while she was busy in her love affair and her new profession of journalist, Sido was dying. She had been failing for some time, but, refusing to accept this, had neglected to husband her strength. In *La Maison de Claudine* Colette tells how Sido would be found moving furniture, sawing logs in the yard, defying the intimations of mortality she had already received. Now, recognizing

that she had been too busy and too happy to give Sido the
time she longed for, Colette preferred to reverse what had
actually happened and make it seem that it was Sido who
had declined to visit her.

Sido died in September 1912. Colette wrote to Hamel:
'Maman died the day before yesterday. I don't want to attend
the funeral.' (All her life she hated the finality of funerals, as
if by refusing to attend them, she was enabled to keep the
dead person alive in her imagination, to deny the fact of
death.) 'I've told almost no one, and I'm not wearing any
outward mourning. For the time being everything's all right.
But I am tortured by the stupid notion that I won't be able
to write to Mother now as I used to so often . . . My brother
will be very unhappy . . .'

The half-brother Achille, Sido's eldest child, with whom
she had lived after Captain Colette's financial misfortune,
died only fifteen months after his mother. Before doing so,
he destroyed the 3,000 letters Colette had written to Sido.
Was this an expression of resentment?

Two months later Colette became pregnant. She was
thirty-nine. In December de Jouvenel married her; his
mother and sister received her with great kindness at their
château in the Corrèze. Though they can hardly have been
other than disapproving of her antecedents or unaware of
the scandalous rumours that surrounded her, they were
soon conquered by her charm, by her love of life and natural
manners.

She worked through the first months of her pregnancy,
making her last stage appearance for nine years at Geneva,

writing her column in *Le Matin*, scraping out *L'Entrave*. Her social life was so active that she remarked to Hamel, 'If this child is not the most inveterate partygoer, I give up.' Only in the summer of 1913 did she retire to the château to await the birth.

When it came, it was a hard one – thirty hours of labour. Yet if her daughter had been carried, as Sido had carried her, close to the heart, the result was different. Colette was never able to be close to her daughter as Sido had been to her. She had a hint of this early, reflecting that Sido used to watch her sewing and say, 'Whatever you do you'll never look like anything but a boy that's sewing' – now she would say 'You'll never be anything but a writer who has made a child . . .' At first, though, it was different; she had not yet found cause to reproach herself for this year 'of satisfied love that turns you into an idiot', and the baby, given the same pet-name of Bel-Gazou which Sido had applied to her, basked in the sunshine of her mother's happy love, as she was later to be cast into the shadow when that love turned to disillusion. So, at first, Colette was delighted: 'I've been swimming,' she wrote to Hamel in the summer of 1914. 'Bel-Gazou is superb, brown as a pâté en croûte, with muscles like her mother's and very gay . . .' '. . . My daughter is a radiant little heifer, who is like Sidi feature for feature,' she added a couple of years later.

In two years Colette's life had been turned round: the divorced and discredited tumbler had become Mme la Baronne de Jouvenel des Ursins; Missy's lover had been banished for Sidi's wife; the dancer and novelist had become a journalist; the daughter had been transformed into a mother. And in August, as Colette and Bel-Gazou swam from the beaches of Brittany, the world was plunged into war.

CHAPTER FIVE

War and *La Fin de Sidi*

France mobilized on 1 August. Sidi, with a million and a
half Frenchmen, was recalled to the colours, joining his
regiment, the 23rd Infantry, on the important Verdun sector.
Within weeks, soon after the decisive Battle of the Marne,
which saved Paris, Colette was back in the capital, working
as a night-nurse at a school converted into a temporary
hospital. She made an illicit journey to Verdun to see Sidi,
but in 1915 was working as a journalist again, harder than
ever, for *Le Matin* was in a difficult situation, with a large
part of its editorial and reporting staff in the army. Colette
accordingly found that the paper was making greater
demands on her, and her employment became more varied.
In 1915 she was sent to Rome, where Italy was anxiously
debating whether to enter the war. There she was the victim
of an absurd incident which appealed to her sense of humour
and yet also suggested how insecurely she was established.
Sidi's first wife was also in Rome, and continuing to call
herself la Baronne de Jouvenel; when Colette presented
herself at the Hotel Excelsior she was refused admission on

the grounds that she must be an impostor. In July she was in Venice and then Sidi was able to join her on leave for a brief holiday at Cenobbio on Lake Como. In January 1917 they were back in Rome, where Sidi was a delegate at the Allied Conference.

Anything like normal life was impossible, and Colette is less distinct during the war years than at any other period of her life. It is not surprising; she had never taken any interest in public affairs; unlike most French writers she was averse from making public pronouncements. And now the world was dominated by those concerns which had always bored her. She worked as she was asked; she brought up her daughter; she wrote to her friends, among whom Hamel, her closest correspondent for ten years, died in 1917; she worried about Sidi's safety; but the war was always there, and in its inhumanity and destructiveness it was a denial of everything she represented.

It had an effect on her marriage which was to contribute to its breakdown. In July 1917 Sidi became private secretary to an old friend, Anatole de Monzie, who had been appointed an under-secretary in the department of the Mercantile Marine. 'I was the one who turned him away from journalism and lured him to politics,' de Monzie claimed; in doing so, he undermined Colette's marriage: she had been ready and willing to follow Sidi into journalism, but politics closed a door between them. In 1918 Sidi worked on the Disarmament Commission; in 1921 he was elected to the Senate; the following year he served as a delegate to the League of Nations; in 1924 he was Minister of Public

Education under Poincaré; but by that time they had separated.

Politics made impossible the equal partnership which Colette sought. She found herself at dinner parties where she was disregarded. 'I accepted my solitude in the midst of keen masculine conversation with good grace,' she said, and even learned to be grateful to the occasional guest who remembered to praise the lamb or the coffee. All the same she could not hide her dissatisfaction: 'It's a good thing I'm going to meet Carco later this evening in Montmartre,' she told Sidi once, 'I will be able to relax with him, he knows how to talk to women.' More and more, she preferred to slip away and spend the evening with literary and newspaper friends like Francis Carco, Jean Lorrain and Christian Béraud, dancing to accordion music in little bars-cabarets in the Rue de Lappe.

Their relations were exacerbated by money problems – Colette was often broke and de Jouvenel could not live within his considerable income, and a growing sense of incompatibility. If Colette resented Sidi's immersion in politics and refused to try to follow him into that world (which rejected women anyway), he himself resented much about her. He was jealous of her animals – she kept a tiger cat and baby panther for some time in their apartment in the Boulevard Suchet at Auteuil: 'Whenever I enter a room where you are alone with your animals, I always have the feeling I am intruding,' he said; 'one day you'll disappear into the jungle . . .' One catches here an echo of her own observation that 'our perfect companions never have fewer than four feet . . .' As he grew more proper and starchy, he disliked her way of life: 'You can't imagine what it is like living with a woman who always has bare feet,' he said in exasperation.

He was unfaithful, and this pained and angered Colette. At the same time, like many who behave badly in personal and sexual relations, he took a strong line on morality and found more and more in Colette's books to displease him. 'Can't you ever write a book that isn't about love and adultery or rupture or half-incestuous goings on?' he asked, 'Aren't there other things in life?' His exasperation received editorial expression: in 1923 *Le Matin* abruptly cut short the serialization of her novel *Le Blé en herbe*; readers, Colette was told, were offended by her frank treatment of adolescent love. Though de Jouvenel was no longer concerned with the day-to-day running of the paper, it is hard to imagine that he was not consulted.

Before then, however, there had been *Chéri*, and this gave Sidi both a general, and a particular, reason for displeasure. It is a simple story, told with consummate art, its tone set from its first sentence: 'Give it to me, Léa, give me your pearl necklace.' The speaker is a beautiful young man, Chéri; Léa is his middle-aged mistress, a famous courtesan in her youth, now a rich woman. She has 'made' Chéri and revels in her creation. His mother, Charlotte Peloux, however, also a courtesan, but grasping and stingy where Léa is bountiful, is preparing a rich marriage for Chéri. He falls in with his mother's plan, without enthusiasm but without opposing her, for Chéri, like many of Colette's young men, is fundamentally passive. He marries Edmée, but finds no satisfaction in this raw and ignorant girl. He leaves her and spends three months with his friend Desmond, dreaming of Léa. At last he returns and they have one night of perfect love. But, in the morning, as Léa is congratulating herself that he has come back to her, he sees her 'not yet powdered, a meagre twist of hair at the back of her head, double chin, and raddled neck ... exposing herself rashly to the unseen observer'. That glimpse breaks the rapport, though it is some time before both realize it; then, 'Forgive me, Chéri,' Léa says, 'I've loved you as if we were both destined to die in the same hour. Because I was born twenty-four years before you, I was doomed, and I dragged you down with me.' She sends him back to his wife: 'She loves you: it's her turn to tremble; but her misery will come from passion and not from perverted mother-love. And you will talk to her like a master, not capriciously, like a gigolo. Quick, quick, run off ...' Chéri still hesitates: 'He looked even paler when he was dressed, and a halo of fatigue round his eyes made them seem larger ...' But he goes.

She closed the door behind him, and silence put an end to her vain and desperate words. She heard Chéri stumble on the staircase and she ran to the window. He was going down the four steps and then he stopped in the courtyard. 'He's coming back! He's coming back!' she cried, raising her arms. An old woman, out of breath, repeated her movements in the long pier-glass, and Léa wondered what she could have in common with that crazy creature ...

As for Chéri, she sees him 'look up at the spring sky and the chestnut trees in flower, and fill his lungs with the fresh air, like a man escaping from prison'. It is not the last of Chéri; the sequel, written in 1923–4 and published in 1926, will contradict this last sentence and show us Chéri entering a new prison where the gates are double-locked by his past and personality, but, in 1920, Chéri had not yet reached this point and we are left with Léa gazing in anguish after her youthful and departing lover.

Chéri had a great public success. Colette had written from the heart, exquisitely, with great feeling: 'I made up Léa with foreboding. Everything one writes comes to pass . . .' Straight away she dramatized it in collaboration with her friend Léopold Marchand. In 1922 she appeared on the stage herself as Léa in its hundredth performance. This was distasteful enough for de Jouvenel: to have his wife playing a courtesan on stage while he represented his country at the League of Nations. Moreover, *Chéri*'s public success had not been matched with critical acclaim. She herself said, 'At the time of *Chéri*'s success only the women supported me.' This was not quite true: André Gide wrote admiringly of the book. More typical, however, was the attack made by Jean de Pierrefeu in the *Journal des débats*: 'Her art depicts strange, vulgar and boring *milieux* . . . it is time for her to find new characters . . . She has too much genius . . . to persist in slumming.' This exactly reflected Sidi's own opinion; he admired his wife's talents, as he had proved by recruiting her to write for his paper; but he wished she would choose other themes. He had, however, another and even weightier

93

cause for displeasure: *Chéri* gave rise to the most unpleasant rumours.

De Jouvenel had two sons, Bertrand, child of his first marriage, and Renaud, the Panther's boy. Colette set herself to be a good stepmother. Her first care was for Renaud, whom she recognized as 'a child who had been neglected in almost every respect'. She called him 'the Kid' (in English – the Chaplin film with that title was released in 1920), and struck up a happy and joking friendship with him. He came to Rozven to spend summers swimming with Colette and Bel-Gazou, for whom he formed a warm and protective friendship. (Missy had generously let Colette keep the house in Rozven for which she had paid; perhaps she had no choice in the matter, for it had always been in Colette's name, the previous proprietor having refused to sell to Missy because she dressed like a man.)

Claire Boas kept Bertrand from his father and Colette till 1920, when Sidi insisted that he be allowed to pay them a visit, declaring that if Claire refused he would take steps to prevent her from continuing to call herself la Baronne de Jouvenel. Bertrand was almost seventeen, sensitive and highly intelligent. Colette found him 'charming'; he very soon fell in love with his beautiful and remarkable step-mother. When she died he remembered her at Rozven:

Think of a garden in Brittany, by the sea. It is early morning and she has been awakened by the melancholy two-note whistling of those birds we call *courlis* . . . she sits in delightful loneliness on the damp and salty grass and her hand enjoys the roughness of the herbs. The sound of the waves fills her mind, she looks now at them, now at the flowers, which are moving faintly upward as the weight of the dew dissolves. The earthly paradise is here; it is not lost for her; others merely fail to see it, indeed shut themselves out from it. She is completely unconscious of political events, wholly devoid of any ambition; indeed, she is incapable of any planning or scheming in any realm, even to gain or retain any human affection ...

It was Colette who had taught Bertrand to know that earthly paradise; Sidi, with his political ambitions, who had 'shut himself out from it'. Bertrand, even more than forty years later, responded to the idyll which Colette could create in and around herself. He was handsome, young, poetic and impressionable; no wonder he fell in love. As for Colette, she too was soon entranced. She was at that age when youth suddenly becomes a memory and a temptation. In the last few years she had grown fat. She had just written *Chéri*, finished in June 1919, some six months before she first met Bertrand. She had created Léa: 'Everything one writes comes to pass.' In her relationship with Missy she had been simultaneously child and lover; now she could be lover and mother. On the one hand she could find amusement in his serious concerns, as she did not in her husband's: 'Bertrand is eighteen now, and, as is fitting for his age, he has plans to reform the European financial system ...' 'Bertrand is in Paris for a week, the imbecile ... he is organizing some kind of democratic youth group or other fantasy ...' She loved swimming and skiing with him; she relished his devotion: 'Bertrand follows me round like a puppy leopard, a big whippet of a boy ...' On the other hand, he touched her heart. She took him to her mother's house at Saint-Sauveur, and he urged her to write about it. They dashed off to Algeria together. When they reached Marseilles on the return journey the hotels were full, but 'an unexpected departure from the Splendide meant that we could have a twin-bedded room with a bath. We took advantage of both . . .'

No wonder tongues wagged. Were not this fat woman (she was just beginning the menopause, weighed almost thirteen stone and considered that she looked like 'a fat Triton' in her bath) and the handsome youth Léa and Chéri in person? Sylvain Bonmariage, briefly her lover almost twenty years earlier, had no doubt: 'the drama of the divorce' (from Sidi) he wrote in his memoir *Colette Willy et Moi*, 'would be a too delicate matter to mention has not Colette written a too detailed account of it in *Chéri* . . . Léa is Colette, Chéri is Hippolyte. Racine shows us a Phèdre tormented by her guilty love, but it is not incestuous. And nothing happens. The Boulevard Suchet was something else.' Nathalie Clifford Barney was equally certain: she thought that Colette seduced her stepson in order to be revenged on her faithless husband.

It was not so straightforward. Colette undoubtedly loved Bertrand, as Léa loved Chéri; in the end like Léa she would send him away. But those who saw the book as a *roman à clef* are contradicted by the timing. The matter was more remarkable: art anticipated life. Of course, even had this not been so, Chéri is much less than Bertrand de Jouvenel, quite lacking his serious intellectuality and far more self-

ish. But 'I wrote Léa with foreboding' – that was true
enough.

Gossips, however, found the situation of the novel all too
juicily patterned in real life to let the matter drop. Colette
tried to conceal what was happening; she forbade Bertrand
to write to her at *Le Matin* lest the letter fell into Sidi's
hands. Sidi himself was put in a position he found intolerable.
His own infidelity, Colette's fierce jealousy, had already
damaged their marriage. There were family quarrels, 'con-
versations full of hidden meanings, insults, servile pleadings
or slammed doors'. The atmosphere soured as battle raged
between them. Colette had been made miserable by his behaviour; now it was her turn. Moreover, he could not endure
that she should have an existence independent of his, and
his vanity was bruised by the scandals and opprobrium she
attracted. (The wives of his fellow-politicians feared and
disliked her; they were afraid she would seduce their husbands.) He had become more and more certain that she was
an unsuitable wife for a rising politician; and now this.
Moreover, he was still himself pursuing the Princesse Marthe
Bibesco.

According to Bertrand, the crisis was reached one day
in October 1923, during lunch. 'My father announced
that he was sending me to Prague for a training course.
"No," said Colette. "What do you mean, No?" said my
father. "Bertrand will stay with me. I do not want to send
him away ..." '

It was Sidi who left. In December 1923 he walked out of
the Boulevard Suchet; 'without a word when I was on a

97

lecture tour. I am divorcing . . .' In fact proceedings were initiated by de Jouvenel, and Colette and Bertrand remained lovers for two more years. When she sent him away, she turned her back on the most stormy period of her life.

De Jouvenel had walked out, but he continued to occupy Colette's imagination. Seventeen years later she wrote a short novel, which, while not in the strict sense autobiographical, explores her feeling for Sidi. It is called *Julie de Corneilhan*.

Julie, by no means to be identified with Colette, yet resembling her creator in her proud and independent morality, is a woman of fifty who has been married twice. She comes from an impoverished Breton family belonging to the *petite noblesse*. She lives in a studio flat, having 'sacrificed smartness to convenience, a bargain she never ceased regretting, especially on fish days, cabbage days and melon days'. She depends on an allowance from her first husband, and 'her slightly over-done trimness betrayed the fact that Julie de Corneilhan was approaching the age when women decide to sacrifice their face to their figures'. She has a young lover, Coco Vatard, a well-to-do bourgeois whom she rather despises, a little friend called Lucie who plays the piano in a night-club, and a raffish little circle of friends.

She is waiting to go to the cinema with them when her brother Léon arrives. Léon, proud, misanthropic, impecunious, cares only for his horses and his sister. He tells her that her second husband, Herbert d'Espivant, has had a heart attack; since Herbert is a prominent politician, it's in the papers. Julie can't go out to the cinema. She sends her friends away and she and Léon have a frugal supper together.

This first chapter is written with the most perfect economy and exactness; Julie is unmistakably placed by it.

She is then summoned to Herbert's sick-bed, in the absence of his millionaire wife Marianne. He greets her affectionately. 'Round his brown eyes were dark circles; so many women, too many women, had painted them there and loved them.' When he talks about his wife, Julie tells him he behaves 'like a cad to her'. 'No,' he replies, 'I lie to her. I . . . I was a cad to you because I used to tell you the truth.' Now he tells her that he has got nothing from Marianne, none of this wealth is his, he has even declined a dowry. Instead 'She's put all her worldly goods at my disposal. You see the difference . . .' She asks why he married Marianne; to pay for my election expenses is the gist of his reply . . . Marianne's fortune is 'not what you would call "money"; it's a board of directors. It's a labyrinth.'

It is on her second visit that he reveals his plan. Once, before they were married, Julie sold a diamond necklace, given her by her first husband, and handed the money on to Herbert. He gave her a receipt for a million francs. Now he suggests, with subtle indirection, that she should produce the receipt, get the cash from Marianne and split the profit. He is tempting her to join him in a conspiracy against his second wife.

She knows him so well, she sees through him, and so she

feels a reviving tenderness. Asked the other day by an old friend how she gets on with d'Espivant now, she replied, 'We dote on each other as long as we're not married . . .' Now she looks on him and thinks 'it's a disaster'; 'and her eyes grew moist, not with pity, but with regret for the past, for this faithless musketeer of hers with his delicate beauty and his faintly martial pose'. She sees him 'always on the look-out for sensuality, pleasure-blackmail, pleasure-panacea, pleasure-death-blow. Is that all he knows about or understands . . .?'

Then comes the news that Marianne's son, an adolescent called Toni, who has fancied himself in love with Julie, has been discovered unconscious in an hotel. 'A photograph of you,' Herbert says,

was found at his bedside. Also, a letter saying that he was taking his life voluntarily and a note from you putting off a rendezvous. That's all. What have you got to say to all that?'

'Nothing,' Julie said.

He stood up with violence.

'What do you mean, nothing?'

'Ah yes, of course! I'd like to know if you'd have preferred the note from me to have been an acceptance of his rendezvous, instead of a refusal. I didn't put it off. I refused it.'

She felt at the top of her form, a condition of which her moral solitude had long robbed her. Once again she was deep in the atmosphere where women, the permanent objects of men's rivalry, bear all their suspicions light-heartedly, listen to their insults, yield under varied assaults and hold their own against masculine presumption and derive from it a simple and lively pleasure . . . 'He's got no idea what to say or do,' she thought. 'In point of fact, men scarcely ever have . . .'

She points out that Toni is not her type. 'I can't bear adolescents . . .' '. . . She was longing to overstep the mark, to hear insulting words and slamming doors, to twist her wrists free from somebody's hands again – a lover's or a stranger's – to measure her strength against that of another, voluptuously, or in a struggle.' But, 'a generous impulse overcame her' and she asks Herbert if he is really cross . . . 'I'm not going to have you discussing any male creature as if you were deciding to use it or not to use it' he bursts out in reviving jealousy. He insults her and she leaves.

For some days she cannot bring herself to a decision. She broaches the matter to her brother who tells her that 'nothing that puts you in touch with d'Espivant can do you any good . . . because you're so weak . . .' Besides, 'he's such a fool . . . Don't you see he's done nothing but idiotic things all his life – always in a bright and intelligent manner . . .' That is one summing-up, of Henri de Jouvenel as well as of Herbert d'Espivant. Nevertheless Julie gives way. She sends him the receipt with a note saying 'do what you like' and signs it with his pet-name for her, 'Youlka'.

Instead of Herbert, it is Marianne who arrives at Julie's flat. Their conversation is strained, painful and, incidentally, funny. Julie realizes that Herbert has contrived to put her completely in the wrong; it seems as though she has been almost blackmailing him – at a moment when he is in poor health too. But she takes the responsibility, resisting the

101

temptation to expose Herbert. Marianne leaves. Julie waits for Herbert to telephone her to find out how it has gone. Then 'a rough thirst for rescue work, and unquestioning feminine longing to prove her devotion, assailed her ... "you'll have your beastly little million ... And if we pull it off, I won't think twice about whatever share of the loot you throw me ..." ' She decides she will telephone him.

At that moment she observes an envelope lying on the table, addressed to her in Herbert's hand. It contains 100,000 francs. Marianne has paid up and Herbert has passed on her cut: 'It's the last straw of cruelty. It's ... It's ten per cent; what a middle-man or house agent would get ...' Herbert has not even written a line to let her feel they are accomplices ... she has been finally dismissed from his life, with her pay-off. The novel ends with Julie riding down to the country with Léon and his groom. She gives Léon half the money, telling him it's a gift from her first husband Becker.

Julie de Corneilhan is admirable for many reasons; its economy and directness persuade one that we are learning the precise truth about the characters. As always in Colette's fiction the novel is shot through with a visual intensity. Most admirable however is the absence of self-pity. Julie is judged as fairly as d'Espivant. It is a very revealing picture of a relationship between two people who are locked in a struggle for mastery. Neither has been ready to give up the right to independent action. They are both faithless and both reluctant to let go. If these characteristics are more marked in d'Espivant, than in Julie, this is because of the circumstances in which history, society and moral outlook have placed him as a man. Colette accepted that de Jouvenel had made her unhappy; she saw also that the qualities in him which had made this possible were also those which had persuaded her to love him. While passion lasted marriage was bound to involve pain; it could not help being a struggle between two egos. It could only stop being such a struggle when it settled into friendship, or if one partner was prepared to sacrifice his or her individuality to the other. By the time she wrote this novel she had discovered contentment in marriage; she still returned to lick the wounds of her marriage with Sidi; to try to understand it, but not to condemn. Though Herbert behaves badly in this novel, and though he is summed up dismissively by Léon, we never doubt – any more than Julie does – that he was properly the man in her life.

One casualty of the divorce was their daughter. Colette's early delight in Bel-Gazou – 'with her Limousin accent, herding the cows, she's a love' – was tempered by her awareness of her resemblance to Sidi, though that had at first delighted her. Now she moved from 'she's an awfully bossy little Sidi' through humorous resignation – 'Bel-Gazou's questions to me this year are of a depressing banality: "when we get to Paris can I wear long stockings?" ' – to complaints of her 'abominable independence and insolent expression'. Very soon she was saying, 'She's a monster who'll be sent off to school soon, and that's that.' And indeed Bel-Gazou was already dispatched to boarding-school at St-Germainen-Laye in October 1922, more than a year before her father left Colette.

Colette felt guilty, guilty enough to break her unspoken rule and try to justify herself. 'The boarding-school principle is obviously monstrous,' she said, 'but recourse to it is probably henceforth inevitable.' It was better for a child than being raised in an atmosphere of family quarrels ...

Nathalie Clifford Barney judged that 'the growing resemblance between the daughter and the detested husband ... may have been a trial to Colette's feelings ...' Perhaps, but Colette was also unable to equal Sido's self-abnegation, and live for her child. She was capable of great generosity of feeling, but she was also self-centred; perhaps spoiled by Sido, hardened by her experiences of marriage and career, she was accustomed to put herself first. She remained, part of her, always a daughter seeking to be cherished and admired, rather than a mother; it was in the 1920s, when Bel-Gazou was an adolescent, that Colette turned back to write about Sido, and recover the lost time of her own girlhood.

After the divorce, Bel-Gazou was brought up as a de Jouvenel. (Later she called herself 'Colette de Jouvenel'.) She spent part of the summers with her mother. She married, young, briefly and unhappily, seeking a divorce 'for an unimpeachable motive', as her mother put it, 'physical disgust'. She lived in the country, in the château in the Corrèze, and devoted herself to her animals.

There was no breach with her mother. Maurice Goudeket, himself puzzled to determine their relations, wrote:

What seems certain is that, as long as her daughter was very young, Colette showed herself the most attentive and experienced of mothers. But though she did not thrust her child away from her from one day to the next, with the severity of female animals, she thought that after a certain age 'succeeding generations are not made to live together'. She also thought that, if she kept her daughter with her, she would have to choose between her work and her . . .

Yet he also noted that

Every time I saw Colette and her daughter together, they were experiencing the greatest pleasure at being with each other, but where feelings are concerned they both had great shyness, which does not encourage demonstrations, and risks confusing reserve with coldness and discretion with lack of trust. When, for no particular reason, they remained for long months without seeing each other, they regretted it equally. On meeting again they sought for a contact which was never quite established. Happily the years only improved these relations, and at the end mother and daughter came together again . . .

There is a certain reserve in Goudeket's own judgement; not surprisingly; it was hardly conceivable that Bel-Gazou, like most children of broken marriages, did not from time to time resent what had happened, feel deprived of the security to which children know they are entitled, and follow the frequently unjust habit of blaming both parents for their deprivation. Young Renaud de Jouvenel, 'the Kid', who was fond of his half-sister, blamed Colette for neglecting her; and Colette de Jouvenel said once that she found her mother

105

'intimidating'. Even so, had Colette not drawn our attention so compellingly and tenderly to her own relations with Sido, had she not so emphasized the sacred responsibility of mother-love, so insisted on what a mother could be to her daughter, we should not find her relationship with Bel-Gazou in any way remarkable. If we do so, it is because we feel that Colette has no right to be merely ordinary.

CHAPTER SIX

A Writer in Her Fifties

Colette was a few weeks short of her fiftieth birthday when de Jouvenel walked out and left her, for the second time, a woman on her own. She had proved herself a talented and copious journalist; she would still appear for a few more seasons on the stage, playing her own creation Léa (in 1925 at Monte Carlo Marguerite Moreno took the part of Charlotte Peloux); she had written two novels hailed as masterpieces, *La Vagabonde* and *Chéri*; she was broke. This time, however, she was less bruised than when Willy had cast her over. She retained her self-confidence; she knew she could maintain herself. She was hardly nobody now, but one of the best-known writers in France. She had a serious, as well as a scandalous, reputation; in 1920 she had been created a Chevalier de la Légion d'Honneur. Nevertheless, till near the end, her life would illustrate the truth of Anthony Powell's observation that a writer may have his name all over the newspapers, yet be uncertain where his next cheque is coming from.

However, her reaction to her husband's departure was

spirited; she declined to postpone a skiing holiday arranged with Bertrand de Jouvenel, even though she must have been aware of the rumours about them. On that subject she remarked: 'Yes, I knew Chéri; like temptations, there were many of him.'

The break-up of her marriage also ended her connection with *Le Matin*. That was to be expected. Fortunately she found herself in demand: *Le Figaro*, *L'Éclair* and *Le Quotidien* all approached her. Then she settled on another paper, *Le Journal*. Later, in 1929, she would become drama critic of *La Revue de Paris*. Journalism would continue to occupy her till after the Second World War when she became immobile.

She had made up Léa with foreboding, and was playing her on stage, but she was not ready to become her and abandon love, as Léa does in *La Fin de Chéri*, where her clothes proclaim that 'the wearer had abdicated, was no longer concerned to be a woman, and had acquired a kind of sexless dignity'. She was still to form one more relationship; it would last till her death, and would be the happiest and most tranquil she had known.

Maurice Goudeket was sixteen years younger than Colette, but he was no pampered Chéri. He was agreeable-looking rather than handsome, and his ears stuck out (traditionally a sign of courage). His father was half-Dutch, half-French, a dealer in precious stones, his mother Jewish. As a young man Maurice had had literary ambitions; he was a schoolfellow of Jean Cocteau, and discovering Colette's books at the age of fifteen or sixteen told his parents, 'I am going to marry that woman. She is the only one who will be able to understand me . . .' Though he later dignified this with the description of 'premonition', he certainly forgot it in the course of the next two decades. He laid aside his ambition to write after bringing out the obligatory little volume of poems, and went into his father's business, specializing in pearls.

He met Colette for the first time early in 1925, at a dinner party to which she had been brought by Marguerite Moreno. 'She was lying flat on a sofa, dressed in a printed frock. With her head raised, under its crown of dishevelled hair, and her bare arms, whose beautiful modelling at the shoulders struck me, a little too plump moreover, she looked like a large cat stretching herself.' He observed her 'without charity'. When he was placed next to her at table, and she at once took an apple from the basket of fruit and bit hungrily into it, his 'suspicion increased'. He 'thought that she was playing the part of herself'. It was a boring evening. Neither enjoyed it.

A few weeks later he went for a holiday to Cap d'Ail. Colette arrived to stay with the same friends. Without planning to – there was a failure to get a train ticket – they found themselves driving back to Paris together. That journey dissolved suspicions, cemented a friendship. Back in Paris Colette sent him a copy of *La Vagabonde* inscribed 'For Maurice Goudeket, in memory of a thousand miles of vagabondage', and an invitation to lunch. Their long idyll, for it was that, had begun.

For ten years they were lovers who lived nominally apart. They formed the habit of taking adjoining apartments in

Paris, in the Rue de Beaujolais overlooking the Palais-Royal, then in the Hôtel Claridge in the Champs-Élysées. They took 'great trouble to safeguard the proprieties, getting them to put in separate entrances and bells, protecting partitions and separate telephones, all of which cost a considerable amount. After which it occurred to us that it would perhaps have been simpler to marry.'

Even so they did not marry till 1935, and then only because they were planning a trip to New York, where they felt their unmarried state might create difficulties. When they did, it was in a simple ceremony in the *mairie*. Goudeket went to some trouble to keep the occasion secret and exclude the Press. In the end he persuaded the official at the *préfecture* not to publish the banns on the grounds that their neighbours had believed they were already married and that 'it would create a scandal if they were to learn, precisely through your marriage, that you were not . . .' After the brief ceremony they drove out to an inn called Au Père Léopold at Vaux-de-Cernay, where 'there was succulent ham cooked in a *pot-au-feu* with pink fat and crackling and a *bouillon* redolent with nutmeg, celery, horseradish'. It was April, but, as they drove back to Paris, it began to snow, and Colette insisted on stopping the car so that she might stand in the road and let the spring snowflakes fall on her face. She was sixty-three.

From the first, however, they had spent their summers openly together, first in a little house Goudeket owned in Provence called La Bergerie, then in a house Colette bought in St Tropez and re-named La Treille Muscate. It became the best loved of all the places she had lived in since she grew up, and she only left it in 1938 because it had lost the charm of privacy. In the first years though, in those days when few went to the South of France in the heat of summer, she loved it dearly; it is the setting of *La Naissance du jour* (*Break of Day*), the most lyrical of all her works. 'How rich it is,' she wrote,

and what a lot of time I've spent not knowing it! The air is light, the grapes ripen so quickly that they are dried and wrinkled on the vine by the sun, the garlic is highly flavoured. That noble bareness that thirst sometimes confers on the soil, the refined idleness that one learns from a frugal people – for me these are late-discovered riches. But let me not complain. My maturity is the right time for them. My angular youth would have bled at the touch of the striated, mica-spangled rocks, the forked pine-needles, the agave, the spines of the sea urchin, the bitter, sticky cistus and the fig tree, the underside of whose every leaf is a wild beast's tongue. What a country!

Like other lovers of the natural world, Norman Douglas for instance, Colette came back to the ultimate realities of rocks and waters. She might have echoed his summing-up in *Old Calabria*:

A landscape so luminous, so resolutely scornful of accessories, hints at brave and simple forms of expression; it brings us to the ground where we belong; it ministers to the disease of introspection and stimulates a capacity which we are in danger of unlearning amid our morbid hyperborean gloom – the capacity for honest

111

contempt; contempt of that scarecrow of a theory which would have us neglect what is earthly, tangible . . .

It was the miracle of Colette's achievement, manifest in *La Naissance du jour*, that she was able to combine an honest introspection which was not diseased with an intense awareness of the physical world, and the ability to make it real in words; certainly, she would never neglect what was 'earthly, tangible'.

La Naissance du jour is written in a manner she had made her own and of which she had acquired an unparalleled mastery. It is part a novel, part an autobiographical meditation, part a celebration of her house, garden and animals. More perhaps than in any other of her books she is here taking stock. Sido is here again, naturally, as Colette measures her life against that which Sido might have wished for her, and against what Sido's had been. 'Each of us had two husbands, but whereas both of mine – I'm glad to say – are very much alive, my mother was twice widow. Since she was faithful out of tenderness, duty and pride, my first divorce upset her, and my second marriage still more . . .' She had feared that Colette would develop the habit of husbands: 'It's a habit that grows and soon you won't be able to do without it . . .' Yet, though she was writing this book early in her love for Maurice (who is not, however, to be identified with the young lover in the fictional part of the book), Colette here presents herself as coming to the end of love: 'Love, one of the great commonplaces of existence, is slowly leaving mine . . .' 'Autumn is the only vintage time,' she reflects, and then going on to ponder on the matter of love, thinks of autumnal love – 'perhaps that is true of love too. It is the season for sensual affection, a time of truce in the monotonous succession of struggles between equals, the perfect time for resting on a summit where two slopes meet . . .' One does not turn to Colette for systematic thought, but rather for this sort of illuminating apprehension that can hold steady the twin but opposite ideas of the passing of love and its maturity being coincidental.

She was indeed on that summit where two slopes meet. From now on, all her writing, except naturally her journalism, harks back. With *La Fin de Chéri*, she had come up to the year after the war. She had already written of her childhood in *La Maison de Claudine*. With that and the three essay-memoirs, *Sido*, *The Captain* and *The Savage*, and now this evocation of her mother again in *La Naissance du jour* (where, having quoted another letter from Sido, she ends by asking, 'Between us two, which is the better writer, she or I? and answers 'Does it not resound to high heaven that it is she?'), she had paid full tribute to her mother's house. In the next years she would write *Ces plaisirs* (abruptly cut off in its serialization in *Gringoire* on account of its supposed indecency) and then deal with the Willy years in *Mes apprentissages*. In fiction too she was happier to turn back to the past.

Yet she lived very urgently in the present. The slump of 1929 hit Goudeket's business. 'Maurice is broke, cleaned out . . . he has put his tail between his legs and attempted to pick up the pieces . . .' He was unable to do so; like many others in those hard years he had to turn his hand to whatever might bring in some money; in 1933 he was selling washing-machines and a tool for unclogging drains. That was his low spot; afterwards he found a niche in popular journalism, writing for *Paris-Match*, *Marie-Claire* and *Paris-Soir*.

Colette herself was almost swamped by journalism in the thirties. Her years as drama critic were particularly demanding. In one of her recurrent bouts of dissatisfaction with her trade, she attempted an abrupt change of direction and opened a beauty salon, selling products of her own fabrication. Goudeket tried to dissuade her; though he was to say that 'a man does not love a woman because of her genius; he loves her in spite of her genius' – he felt that the time the enterprise would demand would be time taken from her true work. He suggested that her reputation might be hurt; she asked him 'why all tradespeople were not put in prison if I thought it dishonourable to indulge in trade'. He suggested that the middle of a commercial crisis was not the best moment to start such a business, but he gave way, reckoning that if it was successful, she would 'return to her writer's bench with a little less uncertainty for the morrow' while 'a failure, after a few days of disappointment, would be quickly forgotten'.

She enjoyed starting the business, visiting the laboratories, writing advertisements, giving demonstrations in Paris and the provinces. The shop, opened in the Rue de Miromesnil, attracted customers, and Colette found it stimulating to meet them. But the demonstrations attracted people more interested in her books than her beauty products; it was not so easy to give up literature as she had supposed. Moreover, a professional in literature, she was no more than a gifted amateur in her new trade. She had the mark of the amateur, an inability to work to a consistent level. Nathalie Barney cast a sceptical eye on the experiment: 'In an attempt to support the enterprise the famous ageing beauty Cécile Sorel agreed to submit to a treatment, but Colette changed her mind from one eye to another, resulting in an asymmetry that doubled the great actress's age and discouraged further volunteers...'

The enterprise petered out. Yet Goudeket, drawing up the balance sheet, found all was not loss: it

had helped Colette to overcome a moment of distaste for her work as a writer, and at the same time had put her in touch with a numerous public which would give her a chance to find fresh themes. Before long now she was to begin the series of short novels which are so human and so stark. For instance, it may be that the truth of a character like 'the wife of the photographer' owes everything to the time Colette spent among ordinary mortals...

She was as hard-working as any ordinary mortal. Her industry did not flag as she entered her sixties. She had learned too to value her work and to insist that she be paid properly. She believed indeed that most writers were underpaid. When the editor of Les Nouvelles littéraires objected that André Gide only asked a quarter of the price she was demanding for an article, she merely replied, 'That's

115

Gide's fault,' and held out for the figure she had named. She would turn her hand to anything. She went on lecture tours, not only in France but to Austria, Romania, North Africa. She wrote screenplays or the dialogue for films such as Max Ophuls's *Divine*. Her trip to New York was undertaken to report the maiden voyage of the *Normandie* for *Le Journal* (prudent and distrustful, she turned up at the Gare du Nord to catch the boat-train with a large picnic basket containing home-made pâté and a cold chicken; the voyage was enlivened by the presence of the Minister of Commerce, who kept asking the journalists if they had heard whether he was still a minister).

In 1938 she visited Fez to report a murder trial for *France-Soir*. The case had aroused great interest in Paris. A body had been found in a hamper on waste land; the police discovered that it had come from a brothel, where they found a number of other bodies and, also, most horribly, four or five young girls walled up and starving to death, and showing signs of having been tortured. The brothel-keeper, a woman called Moulay Hassan, was charged with the crimes, and this intensified the Press's interest, for she was reputed to have done great things on behalf of the French and the French army at the time of the conquest of Morocco. Colette and Goudeket therefore arrived in Fez full of expectation, and were astonished to discover that nobody there was regarding the case as anything out of the ordinary. They were asked if they had really troubled to come all the way from Paris just for this trial. Didn't they understand? It was an affair of no importance: 'It's only to do with women,' the defending counsel told them. 'They are mountain women, who haven't even got any civil status. A crime? Oh yes, yes, of course! But if it hadn't been for that hamper. A few women more or less! Nobody here pays any attention . . .'

Colette, whose life had been spent establishing her right as a free and independent woman to be treated equally by men, who had advanced from the confinement and dependence which Willy had imposed upon her to the partnership she now enjoyed with Goudeket, was revolted by this attitude: 'They were only women.' She had never been, could never be, political: for her each victory was personal. She could never war against society; a struggle was always with a specific person. Yet she brooded on this line: 'They were only women, mountain women, who haven't even got any civil status . . .' Not even that of a wife.

Honours poured in on her. She was promoted to the rank of Officier de la Légion d'Honneur, then, in 1936, to that of Commandant. The same year she was elected to the Académie Royale de Langue et Littérature de Belgique. 'Celebrity,' Goudeket wrote, 'gradually caught her in its toils . . . Very soon there was no longer an investigation in which Colette was not invited to take part, no jury on which she was not invited to sit. A hundred projects were submitted to her, her post began to grow out of all measure, strangers, professional or just idle, knocked at her door, the pile of books and photographs to be autographed grew higher.'

She had two ramparts against her encroaching and demanding fame. The first was her work. She had, in

Goudeket's phrase, 'all the virtues of the French artisan –
humility, patience, self-exaction, pleasure in a well-finished
article', and work, the necessity of every day proving and
stretching herself, had become the centre of her existence.
She might still groan at the labour it demanded; she could
not live without it. 'Right to the end of her life she sometimes
rang for Pauline. "Pauline, I must work. Give me some
paper." "Madame would do much better to rest. Why does
Madame want to write?" "Why, Pauline, because it's my
job." '

Her second defence lay in the full and now happy life she
had built for herself. After the meannesses and betrayals of
her first marriage, the storms and ill-faith of her second, her
life with Maurice was rich and tranquil. Nathalie Barney
had once said that Colette had two faults: she was suscep-
tible to flattery and hated to be alone. 'But of course,' she
added, 'she never was.' Now she never would be. The fact
that Maurice was sixteen years the younger served her as
reassurance. He was ready to live for her, without sacrificing
his individual life. Hence they lived 'without these
groundless scenes which are daily bread in many house-
holds . . . Every moment that we lived together,' he wrote,
'was a moment of fullness and silent joy.' There is no reason
to question what he says.

Fame had its rewards too. In 1938 they were ready to
move again from the flat in the Rue de Marignan that they
had taken after leaving the Hôtel Claridge. A journalist told
her he knew she liked nothing better than moving house.
Colette was indignant. She burst out ('quite untruthfully',

Goudeket says), that whoever had told him that was a liar. Why, she had only moved house fourteen times; each time under compulsion. 'The proof of that is that when, ten years ago, I lived in the Palais-Royal, I went down on my hands and knees to try to rent the first floor flat, and, if I had been able to get it, I should never have moved again.'

The interview was published in *Paris-Midi*. The next day a letter arrived: 'Madame, I read in *Paris-Midi* that you still long for the first floor of 9 Rue de Beaujolais. I am living in this apartment, and I am quite ready to give it up to you . . .'

So Colette moved back to the Palais-Royal, and was as good as her word. She remained there for the rest of her life.

CHAPTER SEVEN

War and the Last Years

In 1938 Colette first had trouble with the arthritis of the hip that would, in a few years, cripple her and confine her to her apartment. It was a sign that life was drawing in; the ringing of a bell already sounded by other deaths. Willy had died, wretchedly and dishonoured, almost forgotten, in 1931; only Colette's portrait in *Mes apprentissages* would give him a second life. De Jouvenel died in 1935; he too would owe his posthumous survival to the wife he had abandoned. Polaire died in 1939, but Claudine kept her memory alive. Other memories were fading: Missy would kill herself horribly in 1944. Colette's brother Léo died in 1940; he had lived, modest and withdrawn, as a lawyer's clerk in Paris, occupying for half a century the same sixth-floor one-room apartment. In a sense he had never left Sido's garden; he would visit Colette, play Chopin on her piano, and then turn the conversation to Saint-Sauveur, which he called 'down there'. Now he was gone and there was no one with whom she could play 'do you remember?'

Her life had been rich in friendship and still was. Two

younger writers, Hélène Picard and Renée Hamon, were regarded almost as daughters. Hélène had been her secretary at *Le Matin*, and was a poet Colette admired; she placed poetry above prose, as, in her hierarchical scale of values, she placed the cat above the dog. Renée Hamon was a Breton girl, an indefatigable traveller whose work Colette cherished (she was a great lover of travel books) and promoted. Older friends like Marguerite Moreno, Nathalie Clifford Barney ('she's a grand sort'), Francis Carco, Jean Cocteau, Princesse Edmond de Polignac (born heiress to the fortune of the Singer Sewing-machine Company, whom Colette had 'adopted' because she looked like 'a multi-millionaire orphan') were still close to her; there were many others whose names mean nothing to British or American readers, and there was her maid Pauline who came to her from the Limousin as a girl of thirteen and remained with her to the end.

The outbreak of war found Colette and Maurice on holiday at Dieppe. They returned to Paris, to the Palais-Royal, within a few days. Colette set herself, in the manner of French countrywomen in time of danger, to store great quantities of provisions. They were both recruited by the radio-station Paris-Mondial to broadcast to America; they recognized the value of propaganda, though Colette was puzzled by the appointment of the diplomat-dramatist Jean Giraudoux as Minister of Information: 'Curious, there's a writer who most of the time proceeds by negation, defining things and people by what they are not ... and he's the man they choose to inform us.'

In that winter of the Phoney War, Colette, suffering from bronchitis, went to Nice for a few days. She had an experience there which, like the offer of the flat overlooking the Palais-Royal, indicates the respect and affection in which she was held. Coming back from the cinema, she had her bag snatched from her hand. She reported the matter to the police, principally in the hope that they might retrieve her papers, regarding the 3,000 francs as lost. The theft was reported in the papers, and two days later Colette received an envelope containing 3,000 francs and a note saying simply, 'I didn't know it was you . . .'

In the spring they suffered two losses. The cat and the dog died within three months of each other. They had had them both for thirteen years, and after this Colette kept no more animals. The cat, which appears in *La Naissance du jour* and is the original of Saha in *La Chatte*, had had a personality so compelling that Colette found it impossible to replace her. Throughout the rest of her life Maurice would sometimes hear her murmur 'Oh, that cat!' She features in *L'Étoile Vesper* (*The Evening Star*) as 'The Last Cat'. The dog, a black bulldog bitch called Souci, might have had a successor, but Colette feared that her encroaching arthritis would make it impossible for her to give a new dog enough exercise. Rather than delegate that responsibility, she preferred to deny herself another animal. It was another sign that life was drawing its horns in. She had never lived without dogs and a cat before: 'Our perfect companions never have fewer than four feet . . .'

*

With the German troops preparing to enter Paris in June 1940, Colette and Goudeket became part of the exodus from the capital which Colette described as 'France slithering on her own surface'. They went first to Colette de Jouvenel in the Corrèze. In less than a month Colette was anxious to be back in Paris: 'I'm used to spending my wars in Paris,' she said. The return was not easy to achieve. They went first to Lyon and from there tried to cross into the Occupied Zone. The German officer at the first crossing point identified first Colette, then Pauline, as Jewish. When Maurice assured him that he alone of the party was of Jewish birth, they were turned back. Three weeks later they tried again, this time armed with a letter of recommendation from the (neutral) Swedish consulate. Arriving in Paris, Maurice, exhausted, failed to stop at a red light. He explained to the policeman that he had driven a long way. 'Oh well,' said the policeman, 'in that case you may not know that we have visitors. So a word of advice . . . walk on tiptoe . . .'

Installed in Paris, Colette would not leave the city again till the war was over. She had her bed moved against the window in their first-floor flat, so that she might look out on the gardens of the Palais-Royal, and share, as far as possible, in the daily struggle of those who lived in her *quartier*. In 1942 she would publish *De ma fenêtre*, meditative notes on what she saw down there. She spent a lot of time in the gardens themselves, talking with the old people and the children, the shopkeepers and the prostitutes. She continued, always, to work. While staying with her daughter she had written:

No matter how ingrained our job is, nor for how long we have done it, it leaves us when an honour, a disaster, or an exodus, involving a whole nation, sweeps us up in its ground-swell ... But at the end of a long road it comes back. I did not foresee that I should travel so far to come up against a table – boundary, obstacle, reef; on legs like stilts, low enough for a bed-table, or wobbly as the pedestal table of a hotel – against a writing-table. Every sight I see provokes me to the same duty, which is perhaps merely a temptation: to write, to depict ...

Even in wartime, in anxiety and ill-health: to write, to depict, what she saw outside her window, what she remembered, what her imagination created. Throughout the war, stories, essays, memories were given written form.

She had cause for anxiety. Maurice was Jewish. That was enough, apart from the general situation of France ... The blow fell on 12 December 1941, at 7.20 in the morning. Pauline awakened Maurice with the news that the Germans had come to arrest him. He sent Pauline to warn Colette but she found her already up. She helped her husband pack his bag and kissed him good-bye, as he went ... neither knew where.

Colette exercised great self-control, showing that stoicism in the face of adversity which was her essence. Impulsive in love, easily upset by small things, she knew how to hold on when others might have given way; she could endure; like Saha, *La Chatte*, 'her patience was that of all those who are wearied out and sustained by a promise'.

She worked to have him released, approaching Germans

and collaborators. She may have thought herself ready to promise anything, but she was brought up short by her inescapable sense of moral propriety, that is to say, of honour. One Frenchman, a writer who had been imprisoned and released when he promised full collaboration, assured her that he could see Maurice safe. He could fix him with a job in the camp at Compiègne which would protect him. All he would have to do would be 'merely from time to time to give a few pieces of information about his fellow-inmates. You see, it's a post of trust,' the man said. Colette refused, and repeated her refusal even when told that the alternative would be death . . .

In fact the alternative was not death. Goudeket was released in February 1942 (through the intervention, it seems, of the Spanish ambassador). He had been lucky in the time of his arrest; eighteen months later and it would undoubtedly have been the death camps. As it was, Colette never fully recovered from this experience. She had been unable to sleep; her nerves had been destroyed. The months after his return were continually disturbed by rumours of mass arrests. In the end Goudeket thought it wiser to slip out of Paris and out of the Occupied Zone. When, after the Allied landings in North Africa, the Germans occupied the whole country, he decided he would be as safe in Paris as anywhere. For the next eighteen months he lived in hiding in the Rue de Beaujolais, spending the nights in an improvised chamber under the roof.

In the midst of these terrible years of fear and privation, Colette's imagination flew back to the past, and she wrote her last little masterpiece of fiction. *Gigi* is the most charming of her works, later to be filmed and made into a musical. She turned back to the *belle époque*, to those days recalled by Nathalie Barney as 'the time of carriages in the Bois de Boulogne . . . when there was an opportunity to exchange long glances, half-smiles, as one drove from the Tir aux Pigeons to the Cascade, passing and passing again most of the fashionable courtesans, actresses, society women and *demi-mondaines*; none of whom had a glance as lovely as Colette's . . .' No wonder Colette reverted to those days for the setting of her little fairy-tale of the girl brought up by her grandmother and great-aunt (the latter modelled partly on Liane de Pougy, who, in her moments of relaxation, had been Nathalie Barney's lover) to be the mistress of the rich sugar-manufacturer Gaston. Gigi, who falls deeply in love with Gaston, is at first dismayed by what her relatives have planned for her, if only because she does not want to abandon her childhood, then falls in with their plan rather than risk losing her Ton-ton, only to find a happy ending opening as Gaston says to her grandmother, 'Mamita, will you do me the honour, the favour, give me the infinite joy of bestowing on me the hand . . .'; with which words the little novel, distinguished by its having no superfluous scene, sentence or even word, ends . . . with a vision of happiness and love.

Colette and Maurice had heard the story of Gigi some fifteen years earlier at a hotel in a suburb of Saint-Raphaël. The girl was the niece of the two ladies who kept the hotel, one of whom was a retired opera singer (Gigi's mother works in the Opéra-Comique, having failed in the profession of courtesan). It had all happened recently, but Colette, having brooded on the story these last fifteen years, was right to set it back in her own youth. The *belle époque* was far enough removed from the realities of the 1940s to have taken on the quality of a fairy-tale time; the atmosphere which now surrounded it softened the harsh mercenary edges of Gigi's story. This decision was an example of Colette's literary tact. Moreover, in turning back to the nineties, to those glittering years of her unhappy first marriage, Colette made her final peace with her own past. *Gigi* emphasizes the sovereignty of the creative imagination. One would never guess the circumstances in which it had been written; it sparkles with humour, irony, love and the affectionate observation of objects and manners; yet its author was old, arthritic, made anxious and unhappy by her fear.

Paris was liberated on 24 August 1944. Colette described the evening as one 'when night rose up like a dawn'. Yet, hearing continued firing the next morning, she told Maurice that she would not believe they were really liberated till he brought her a Scottish major. 'In a kilt?' 'Certainly in a kilt.' He obliged her by doing so. The major stayed to lunch. 'My wife reads a lot,' he said, 'I expect she'll have heard of you.'

If she hadn't, she soon would. Colette was entering the period of her greatest fame. The cause was partly reverence for old age, partly nostalgia: in the grim uneasy deprived years after the war, it was comforting to look back to the *belle époque*, to read someone who magically evoked the pleasures of the senses, whose books fed the imagination with the delights of the garden and the table; above all, perhaps, to turn to a writer who proclaimed the supreme importance of the private life, the individual sensibility.

In 1945 she became the first woman to be elected to the Académie Goncourt; in 1949 its President. (Since she was now usually confined to her bed, the Académie would meet in her room.) In 1948 publication of her *Complete Works*, edited by Goudeket, began; it would run to fifteen volumes. 'Did I really write all that?' she would say as they looked over newspaper articles, previously uncollected, to decide what should be included. Films were made of her books: *Gigi* in 1948, *Julie de Corneilhan* in 1949, with France's greatest actress Edwige Feuillère in the name part, *Chéri* the following year, *La Seconde* in 1951. That year too an adaptation of *Gigi*, made by Anita Loos, opened on Broadway. The play had not been cast when Colette and Maurice went to Monte Carlo in the spring. They found a film being shot in the foyer of the Hôtel de Paris: 'We stopped to gaze at a charming and very young English girl who under the light of the projectors was struggling half in English and half in French. Hardly had Colette watched her perform for a moment than she turned to me and said: "There is our Gigi in America. Don't let's look any further." ' It was Audrey Hepburn, then an unknown with no stage experience . . .

They spent part of the year at Monte Carlo, in a ground-floor suite in the Hôtel de Paris or at Deauville, where Colette, who could no longer tolerate the heat of the South, was happy as long as she could circulate in her wheelchair. But their base was Paris and the beloved flat overlooking the gardens of the Palais-Royal. There she received a constant stream of visitors, old friends and new admirers. These included Elizabeth, the Queen-Dowager of Belgium, who, having enjoyed Pauline's peasant cassoulet, once said she would like to give Colette a present, and asked her to choose what she would like; she requested a bottle of Kriek-Lambik, a strong beer made from cherries which was sold in bars in the poor quarters of Brussels. Colette had enjoyed it in her music-hall days, and now a car came from the Belgian Embassy with half a dozen bottles of what Maurice described as 'this unspeakable beverage'.

Honours continued to flow in: she was made a Grand Officier de la Légion d'Honneur; the city of Paris awarded her its Grande Médaille de la Ville; she received a diploma from the National Institute of Arts and Letters of the United States. She was seen in France as, in Raymond Mortimer's words, 'a national glory, something to enjoy as well as to be proud of, like Chambertin or the Luxembourg Gardens or the Provençal spring'; she would have liked his chosen comparisons.

She continued to work, from her bed which she called 'her raft'. *Le Fanal bleu* (1949) was a work in the same style as *De ma fenêtre* and *L'Étoile Vesper*, a unique blend of observation, memory and meditation. The Swiss publisher Mermod conjured another book from her. Every week for a year or so, he sent her some flowers: 'When you feel like it, you will trace a portrait of one of those flowers. Then we will make a little volume of them.' The result was *Pour un herbier*, illustrated by Raoul Dufy.

But she was fading fast and suffering the pains and losses of old age. Marguerite Moreno died in 1948. Colette wrote to Jean Cocteau: 'To you I can tell the truth – that I don't know when I shall get used to her dying . . . fifty-four years of friendship . . .'

Without animals, without health, with failing power and fewer old friends, it was a matter of preparing to die. She declined sedatives. 'Aspirin changes the colour of my thoughts. It makes me gloomy, I would rather suffer cheerfully . . . Besides I want to know just how far I can go . . .' Her unresting curiosity was turned on her own body and the pain it was experiencing. She depended ever more on Maurice and Pauline. In the summer of 1954 she weakened perceptibly, sleeping long periods, no longer able to read though she still liked to look, through her magnifying glass, at books with pictures of plants, birds and insects or at a collection of butterflies from the Amazon. Her last word to Maurice was 'Look.'

She died, very gently, on 3 August 1954. She had never been a believer, but there was anger and disapproval when the Archbishop of Paris, Cardinal Feltin, declined to permit a religious ceremony at her funeral; Graham Greene wrote a letter of protest. Instead she was given a secular State funeral, and buried in that most beautiful and evocative of cemeteries, Père Lachaise. A huge crowd attended the funeral; many, perhaps the majority, were the ordinary working-women of Paris.

CHAPTER EIGHT

After Words

The 'tumbler' had become President of the Académie Goncourt and a Grand Officier de la Légion d'Honneur; the girl who, in marrying Willy, had given way to 'an atrocious impure adolescent impulse' and who, as Missy's lover, had scandalized even Montmartre, had ended by speaking for millions of Frenchwomen; the girl who had no thoughts of being a writer came to be regarded as a classic in her own lifetime. The bourgeoise, with her mascara, her cats, her little bulldogs, her collection of glass paperweights, was also a countrywoman with a profound knowledge of the garden and the kitchen, and a deep feeling for wild nature. She had, in a remarkable manner, by remaining always true to her own instincts, made her own life, and convinced other women that they could do so too.

The Spanish philosopher José Ortega y Gasset suggested that man, having gone beyond 'such actions as are necessary for existence in nature', might be seen as a 'sort of novelist of himself who conceives the fanciful figure of a personage with its unreal occupations and then, for the

COLETTE

sake of converting it into reality, does all the things he does
– and becomes an engineer ...' Ortega meant this as a
general statement expressing a truth applicable to all human
beings once they pass beyond the natural state of primitive
man, and enter into self-consciousness. It obviously applies
more strongly, the more self-consciousness is developed or
cultivated. Colette, without in any way relaxing her intense
grip of the physical world, carried self-consciousness to the
point when she became very clearly Ortega's 'novelist and
engineer' of her own self.

Her autobiographical works may be taken as material for
her own biography, as I have taken them, but they are also
works of fiction. What is the difference between Sido and
the narrator's grandmother in *À la recherche du temps
perdu*? Is not Willy a fictional character of the same order
as Charlus? Is not the young Colette herself a more vivid
character than Claudine or Proust's narrator? To put these
questions is to enter that misty landscape where memory,
imagination and invention meet and intertwine. Colette was
aware of this – her art is never haphazard.

In *La Naissance du jour* she wrote that

an age comes when the only thing that is left for a woman is to
enrich her own self. She hoards and reckons up everything, even
to blows and scars – a scar being a mark which she did not carry
at birth, an acquisition. When she sighs, 'Oh, what a lot of sorrows
He endowed me with!' she is, in spite of herself, weighing the value
of the word – the value of the gifts. Little by little she stows them
tranquilly away. But there are so many of them that in time she is
forced, as her treasure increases, to stand back a little from it, like

a painter from his work. She stands back, and returns, and stands back again, pushing some scandalous detail into place, bringing into the light of day a memory drowned in shadow. By some unhoped-for art she becomes – equitable. Is anyone imagining as he reads me, that I'm portraying myself? Have patience: this is merely my model.

Since all Colette's books are works of art, not one is true to life. Instead they are true of life. No art can, as Henry James put it, 'compete with life'. 'Life,' Stevenson said, 'imposes by brute energy, like inarticulate thunder; art catches the ear, among the far louder noises of experience, like an air artificially made by a discreet musician.' Colette is such a musician. Stevenson continues:

A proposition of geometry does not compete with life; and a proposition of geometry is a fair and luminous parallel for a work of art. Both are reasonable, both untrue to the crude fact; both inhere in nature, neither represents it. The novel, which is a work of art, exists, not by its resemblances to life, which are forced and material, as a shoe must still consist of leather, but by its immeasurable difference from life, which is designed and significant, and is both the method and meaning of the work.

In short, life is senseless and shapeless; a work of art gives it sense (significance) and a pleasing shape. Yet, at the same time, the work of art itself becomes senseless, if it loses, or over-loosens, its connections with life. The triumph of Colette's art is that this connection is never broken, never even threatened.

She contrives to be at the same time subjective and

133

objective; writing is for her a re-creation in her imagination and on paper of what happens 'out there'. All her books are intensely personal, in that we never cease to be aware of Colette herself (which was why her readers thought of her as a friend and a guide); yet her pure fiction has also a crystalline hardness and objectivity. She might be both Léa and Chéri, but *La Fin de Chéri* has the detachment from personality of a precious stone. It is a novel which draws attention to one other aspect of Colette: that she was a Dandy.

The Dandy insists that life itself can be transformed into art by an exercise of the will; he is, self-consciously, Ortega's novelist-man. All the photographs of Colette show her Dandy awareness of self. She presented a deliberately chosen picture. Goudeket tells us of her 'huge domed forehead, like Beethoven's', which she would never agree to show and which is indeed revealed in only one photograph taken by the American Penn for *Vogue*. 'One cannot say,' Goudeket observes, 'that the picture resembles her. It is without sex, whereas Colette remained feminine to her last breath. The charm, the amiability, the tender irony which characterized her are missing from it. It is, in reality, a photograph of *the other*, of the hidden being which each of us carries within ourself, of the one alone who was able to write certain pages of Colette.' But all the other photographs, even those where she appears most natural, perhaps indeed especially those, reveal a Colette who knows what she is presenting to the world, and who has chosen what she will present.

Chéri, that creation who recalls her own pictures in dinner-jacket and stiff shirts, is a Dandy too, and he is broken by life precisely because it will not fit itself into the work of art which he would make it. He realizes that he has glimpsed perfection in his love for Léa, and that it cannot be repeated; Léa, like life, has changed and moved on. For some weeks he forms the habit of going to the rooms of a woman known as 'the Pal', a broken-down music-hall artiste, who has known Léa in her youth and who will talk to him of her . . . Her conversation is like a drug restoring to him that 'enclosed Paradise in which Léa and Chéri had lived for so many years'. It is an illusion. 'When you sent me away, my Nounoune,' he says, addressing an absent and therefore imaginary Léa by her pet name,

what did you think there was left for me after you? . . . we've been well punished, you and I: you, because you were born so long before me, and I, because I loved you above all women. You're finished now, you have found your consolation – and what a disgrace that is! – whereas I . . . As long as people say 'There was the War' I can say 'There was Léa'. Léa, the War . . . I never imagined I'd dream either of them again, yet the two together have driven me outside the times I live in. Henceforth, there is nowhere in the world where I can occupy more than half a place . . .

Colette gave a prosaic account of her intentions in depicting Léa and Chéri:

I merely wanted to say that when a woman of a certain age has an affair with a very young man, she is in less danger than he of being marked by the experience afterward. No matter what he does, in all his subsequent liaisons, he will be unable to keep from remembering his old mistress . . .

No doubt true; but *La Fin de Chéri* cannot be read without the realization that the matter goes deeper. Chéri is destroyed, brought to shoot himself, because in his affair with Léa, he has glimpsed the ideal, which being only a Dandy and not a Dandy-artist, he cannot re-create. In his lack of will and energy, his inability to make anything of his life, he recalls Saki's Comus Bassington, and indeed the hard brittleness of that remarkable novel, *The Unbearable Bassington*, reveals the same world as is portrayed in *La Fin de Chéri*. (Colette would have appreciated the sentence: 'Francesca, if pressed in an unguarded moment to describe her soul, would probably have described her drawing-room.') Chéri represents for Colette, as Comus does for Saki, the acceptance of the fact that beauty and charm are not in themselves sufficient to ensure happiness. She had recognized that it was 'the duty of the androgynous person never to be happy', and, both in biographical sketches and in her fiction, she had revealed their tragedy, but Colette was herself too sturdily Burgundian, too much her mother's daughter, and finally, too great an artist, to settle for the fate of a Renée Vivien or a Chéri. In the end she was as tough and triumphant as Léa; in the end her art celebrates the endurance of women and, indeed, of humanity.

She was in every way a self-made woman. In the normal sense of the expression, she fought her way from dependence, insecurity and poverty to independence, prosperity and admiration. In a secondary, but even more important sense, she created for herself the character and myth of Colette, and lived them. In the course of her journey she played the loving daughter, the oppressed wife, the free spirit, the challenging lesbian, the passionate wife of a jealous and wilful husband, the divorced woman, the mother, the partner in an equal and happy marriage, the peasant, the bourgeoise, finally the institution that France recognized simply as Colette. She played them all with conviction and style, as she played her parts on the stage. But she never surrendered her individuality, once she had recognized it; she remained always Colette, as a cat is always a cat.

It was her achievement, in a society dominated by men and male values, to insist on her independence as a woman, to claim freedom, while remaining feminine; to assert her equality without ever imitating or denying men. She wrote tenderly, with complete understanding of women, but no other woman has written as well, as compassionately, or, again, with as much understanding, of men; the androgynous element in her own nature, which she recognized and cherished, enabled her to bridge the divide between the sexes. Herbert d'Espivant is treated with the same justice as Julie de Corneilhan, Chéri as Léa; in time she was even able to forgive, and work to an understanding of, Willy.

As an artist she was limited. She never tried to write

beyond her own time and her own experience of life. Having no interest in public affairs or general questions, she ignored them in her fiction and autobiographical essays. Her characters are never troubled by questions of religious faith or political commitment. She knew the limits of her genius and never ventured beyond her own imaginative knowledge. She was reproached for her concentration on a narrow and meretricious world. It didn't worry her. She knew that the criticism was worthless. In the second volume of his memoirs Anthony Powell tells of an encounter with Rose Macaulay, when 'referring to some recently published novel – possibly Waugh's *A Handful of Dust* (1934) – she said to me: "I have not read it yet. Not a very interesting subject – adultery in Mayfair." "Why should you think that an uninteresting subject?" "You are quite right," she said. "It was a silly thing to say. Subjects are entirely a matter of how they are treated by the writer." ' Colette knew – and her work confirms – the truth of that judgement. Léa and Chéri may seem worthless persons, of no social value, their milieu trivial in its concerns, intellectually barren, morally despicable. The three sisters in *Le Toutounier* may appear pathetic in the gallantry with which they confront life. Julie and Herbert d'Espivant may have little to commend them beyond the swagger and courage with which they face the world; Alain, in *La Chatte*, is a feeble mollycoddle. And so on; there is hardly a character in her writings of whom a moralist would approve.

It does not matter. Her subject is first and always the heart, its vagaries, its wilful self-deception, its gallantry, the pain it suffers and the joy it experiences. No one has written better about such matters; as a poet of love she surpasses Proust because she is shackled by no theory insisting that love is always doomed since it always creates an imaginary person, from which ideal the real object of love falls invariably short. Colette knew the partial truth of this, as she knew that love cannot exist without pain and even the desire to hurt, but she knew also that a fusion between the real and ideal, the body and the spirit, could be achieved. And she had learned from her cat that love can escape from the desire for domination.

As she recognized the cruelty of love and yet remained its poet, so she was never blind to the cruelty of the natural world, yet never ceased to celebrate its beauty and wonder. She sought and found harmony between human beings and their natural environment. 'Look,' she said as her last word; and, under her dying breath, one can catch the whisper of a final instruction, 'Marvel and understand.'

With her eye for detail and her quick senses, she celebrated every manifestation of the natural world, without feeling, rooted in the Burgundian earth as she was, any need to seek a transcendental explanation. She had no fear of death, scarcely any curiosity. In *La Naissance du jour* she had asked:

Will my own final lot be that of a light friable body, hollow bones and a great devouring sun over it all? Sometimes I force myself to think of it so as to persuade myself that the second half of my life is making me take a little more thought and care for what happens after . . . the illusion soon passes. Death does not interest me – not even my own . . .

Goudeket says she had no belief in survival after death –

For Colette, it would have meant admitting a fundamental difference between animals and men, which she saw no reason to believe, not that such a difference would necessarily be in man's favour . . .

One sort of survival was granted her. She still lives in her books. For this she suffered much, enjoyed much. Her lover and stepson, Bertrand de Jouvenel, in a note written after her death, observed:

Love has two faces, *agape* and *eros*, a deep understanding and a petulant wilfulness to seize it. It is not easy to divorce them: Colette was immensely rich in the former and therein lies her greatness; for the latter she suffered ample retribution . . .

But without that wilfulness and that suffering, she would not have succeeded in making herself Colette.

Colette's complete works (*Oeuvres Complètes*) began to be published by Le-Fleuron-Flammarion in 1948; the edition runs to fifteen volumes. Previously her works had appeared from a variety of publishing houses.

Her work has appeared in English in a variety of editions and translations. However, Martin Secker & Warburg published all the principal works in the 1950s, and they have since been published in the United States by Farrar, Straus. Many of them have been reprinted in paperback. I have used the Penguin editions of the *Claudine* books, *Chéri* and *The Last of Chéri*, *My Apprenticeships*, *The Pure and the Impure*, *The Vagabond*, *The Captive*, *Ripening Seed*, *My Mother's House* and *Sido*, *Gigi* and *The Cat*, *Chance Acquaintances* and *Julie de Corneilhan*. *Break of Day*, *Duo* and *Le Toutounier* are all published by The Women's Press, also from the Secker & Warburg translations from the Fleuron editions. The *Collected Stories* were published by Penguin in 1985.

The most comprehensive biography is by Michèle Sarde, translated by Richard Miller (Morrow 1980, Michael Joseph 1981). It is strongly feminist in tone and somewhat given to speculation but indispensable. Joanna Richardson's *Colette* (Methuen 1983, Franklin Watts 1984) is an admirably clear and sympathetic portrait. Other biographies include *Colette* by Elaine Marks, originally published in 1960, reprinted by Greenwood Press in 1982. There are critical studies: *The Woman, The Writer*, ed. E. M. Eisinger and M. McCarty (Pennsylvania State University Press 1982) and *Colette* by Joan Hinde Stewart (G, K. Hall 1983). There is also a lavishly illustrated pictorial biography by Genevieve Dormann, *Colette Amoureuse*, translated as *A Passion for Life* (Thames and Hudson 1985).

A selection of Colette's letters, edited by Robert Phelps, was published by Virago in 1982. Robert Phelps also compiled *Belles Saisons: A Colette Scrapbook* (Penguin).

Maurice Goudeket's invaluable memoir *Près de Colette* was published by Flammarion in 1956, and in an English translation by Enid McLeod as *Close to Colette* by Martin Secker & Warburg in the following year. Sylvain Bonmariage's *Colette Willy et Moi* is hostile, unreliable but interesting.

There has been much admirable writing on Colette in magazines and periodicals. Bertrand de Jouvenel wrote a piece in *The Listener* on the occasion of her death from which I have quoted. Some of the Penguin editions contain admirable critical introductions, reprinted either from earlier editions or taken from other sources, by Roger Senhouse, Raymond Mortimer and Janet Flanner.

INDEX

A CHOICE OF PENGUINS

☐ *The Complete Penguin Stereo Record and Cassette Guide*
Greenfield, Layton and March £7.95

A new edition, now including information on compact discs. 'One of the few indispensables on the record collector's bookshelf' – *Gramophone*

☐ *Selected Letters of Malcolm Lowry*
Edited by Harvey Breit and Margerie Bonner Lowry £5.95

'Lowry emerges from these letters not only as an extremely interesting man, but also a lovable one' – Philip Toynbee

☐ *The First Day on the Somme*
Martin Middlebrook £3.95

1 July 1916 was the blackest day of slaughter in the history of the British Army. 'The soldiers receive the best service a historian can provide: their story told in their own words' – *Guardian*

☐ *A Better Class of Person* **John Osborne** £2.50

The playwright's autobiography, 1929–56. 'Splendidly enjoyable' – John Mortimer. 'One of the best, richest and most bitterly truthful autobiographies that I have ever read' – Melvyn Bragg

☐ *The Winning Streak* **Goldsmith and Clutterbuck** £2.95

Marks & Spencer, Saatchi & Saatchi, United Biscuits, GEC . . . The UK's top companies reveal their formulas for success, in an important and stimulating book that no British manager can afford to ignore.

☐ *The First World War* **A. J. P. Taylor** £4.95

'He manages in some 200 illustrated pages to say almost everything that is important . . . A special text . . . a remarkable collection of photographs' – *Observer*

A CHOICE OF PENGUINS

☐ ***Man and the Natural World*** **Keith Thomas** £4.95

Changing attitudes in England, 1500–1800. 'An encyclopedic study of man's relationship to animals and plants . . . a book to read again and again' – Paul Theroux, *Sunday Times* Books of the Year

☐ ***Jean Rhys: Letters 1931–66***
·**Edited by Francis Wyndham and Diana Melly** £4.95

'Eloquent and invaluable . . . her life emerges, and with it a portrait of an unexpectedly indomitable figure' – Marina Warner in the *Sunday Times*

☐ ***The French Revolution*** **Christopher Hibbert** £4.95

'One of the best accounts of the Revolution that I know . . . Mr Hibbert is outstanding' – J. H. Plumb in the *Sunday Telegraph*

☐ ***Isak Dinesen*** **Judith Thurman** £4.95

The acclaimed life of Karen Blixen, 'beautiful bride, disappointed wife, radiant lover, bereft and widowed woman, writer, sibyl, Scheherazade, child of Lucifer, Baroness; always a unique human being . . . an assiduously researched and finely narrated biography' – *Books & Bookmen*

☐ ***The Amateur Naturalist***
Gerald Durrell with Lee Durrell £4.95

'Delight . . . on every page . . . packed with authoritative writing, learning without pomposity . . . it represents a real bargain' – *The Times Educational Supplement*. 'What treats are in store for the average British household' – *Daily Express*

☐ ***When the Wind Blows*** **Raymond Briggs** £2.95

'A visual parable against nuclear war: all the more chilling for being in the form of a strip cartoon' – *Sunday Times*. 'The most eloquent anti-Bomb statement you are likely to read' – *Daily Mail*

CLASSICS IN TRANSLATION
IN PENGUINS

☐ *Remembrance of Things Past* **Marcel Proust**
☐ Volume One: *Swann's Way, Within a Budding Grove* £7.95
☐ Volume Two: *The Guermantes Way, Cities of the Plain* £7.95
☐ Volume Three: *The Captive, The Fugitive, Time Regained* £7.95

Terence Kilmartin's acclaimed revised version of C. K. Scott Moncrieff's original translation, published in paperback for the first time.

☐ *The Canterbury Tales* **Geoffrey Chaucer** £2.95

'Every age is a Canterbury Pilgrimage . . . nor can a child be born who is not one of these characters of Chaucer' – William Blake

☐ *Gargantua & Pantagruel* **Rabelais** £3.95

The fantastic adventures of two giants through which Rabelais (1495–1553) caricatured his life and times in a masterpiece of exuberance and glorious exaggeration.

☐ *The Brothers Karamazov* **Fyodor Dostoevsky** £4.95

A detective story on many levels, profoundly involving the question of the existence of God, Dostoevsky's great drama of parricide and fraternal jealousy triumphantly fulfilled his aim: 'to find the man in man . . . [to] depict all the depths of the human soul.'

☐ *Fables of Aesop* £1.95

This translation recovers all the old magic of fables in which, too often, the fox steps forward as the cynical hero and a lamb is an ass to lie down with a lion.

☐ *The Three Theban Plays* **Sophocles** £2.95

A new translation, by Robert Fagles, of *Antigone, Oedipus the King* and *Oedipus at Colonus*, plays all based on the legend of the royal house of Thebes.

CLASSICS IN TRANSLATION
IN PENGUINS

☐ *The Treasure of the City of Ladies*
Christine de Pisan   £2.95

This practical survival handbook for women (whether royal courtiers
or prostitutes) paints a vivid picture of their lives and preoccupations
in France, *c.* 1405. First English translation.

☐ *La Regenta* **Leopoldo Alas**   £10.95

This first English translation of this Spanish masterpiece has been
acclaimed as 'a major literary event' – *Observer*. 'Among the select
band of "world novels" ... outstandingly well translated' – John
Bayley in the *Listener*

☐ *Metamorphoses* **Ovid**   £2.95

The whole of Western literature has found inspiration in Ovid's
poem, a golden treasury of myths and legends that are linked by the
theme of transformation.

☐ *Darkness at Noon* **Arthur Koestler**   £2.50

'Koestler approaches the problem of ends and means, of love and
truth and social organization, through the thoughts of an Old Bolshe-
vik, Rubashov, as he awaits death in a G.P.U. prison' – *New States-
man*

☐ *War and Peace* **Leo Tolstoy**   £4.95

'A complete picture of human life;' wrote one critic, 'a complete
picture of the Russia of that day; a complete picture of everything in
which people place their happiness and greatness, their grief and
humiliation.'

☐ *The Divine Comedy: 1 Hell* **Dante**   £2.25

A new translation by Mark Musa, in which the poet is conducted by
the spirit of Virgil down through the twenty-four closely described
circles of hell.

A CHOICE OF PENGUINS

☐ *Small World* **David Lodge** £2.50

A jet-propelled academic romance, sequel to *Changing Places*. 'A new comic débâcle on every page' – *The Times.* 'Here is everything one expects from Lodge but three times as entertaining as anything he has written before' – *Sunday Telegraph*

☐ *The Neverending Story* **Michael Ende** £3.95

The international bestseller, now a major film: 'A tale of magical adventure, pursuit and delay, danger, suspense, triumph' – *The Times Literary Supplement*

☐ *The Sword of Honour Trilogy* **Evelyn Waugh** £3.95

Containing *Men at Arms, Officers and Gentlemen* and *Unconditional Surrender*, the trilogy described by Cyril Connolly as 'unquestionably the finest novels to have come out of the war'.

☐ *The Honorary Consul* **Graham Greene** £2.50

In a provincial Argentinian town, a group of revolutionaries kidnap the wrong man . . . 'The tension never relaxes and one reads hungrily from page to page, dreading the moment it will all end' – Auberon Waugh in the *Evening Standard*

☐ *The First Rumpole Omnibus* **John Mortimer** £4.95

Containing *Rumpole of the Bailey, The Trials of Rumpole* and *Rumpole's Return*. 'A fruity, foxy masterpiece, defender of our wilting faith in mankind' – *Sunday Times*

☐ *Scandal* **A. N. Wilson** £2.25

Sexual peccadillos, treason and blackmail are all ingredients on the boil in A. N. Wilson's new, *cordon noir* comedy. 'Drily witty, deliciously nasty' – *Sunday Telegraph*

A CHOICE OF PENGUINS

☐ *Stanley and the Women* **Kingsley Amis**   £2.50

'Very good, very powerful . . . beautifully written . . . This is Amis
père at his best' – Anthony Burgess in the *Observer*. 'Everybody
should read it' – *Daily Mail*

☐ *The Mysterious Mr Ripley* **Patricia Highsmith**   £4.95

Containing *The Talented Mr Ripley, Ripley Underground* and
Ripley's Game. 'Patricia Highsmith is the poet of apprehension' –
Graham Greene. 'The Ripley books are marvellously, insanely read-
able' – *The Times*

☐ *Earthly Powers* **Anthony Burgess**   £4.95

'Crowded, crammed, bursting with manic erudition, garlicky puns,
omnilingual jokes . . . (a novel) which meshes the real and personal-
ized history of the twentieth century' – Martin Amis

☐ *Life & Times of Michael K* **J. M. Coetzee**   £2.95

The Booker Prize-winning novel: 'It is hard to convey . . . just what
Coetzee's special quality is. His writing gives off whiffs of Conrad, of
Nabokov, of Golding, of the Paul Theroux of *The Mosquito Coast*.
But he is none of these, he is a harsh, compelling new voice' –
Victoria Glendinning

☐ *The Stories of William Trevor*   £5.95

'Trevor packs into each separate five or six thousand words more
richness, more laughter, more ache, more multifarious human-ness
than many good writers manage to get into a whole novel' – *Punch*

☐ *The Book of Laughter and Forgetting*
Milan Kundera   £3.95

'A whirling dance of a book . . . a masterpiece full of angels, terror,
ostriches and love . . . No question about it. The most important
novel published in Britain this year' – Salman Rushdie

A CHOICE OF PENGUINS

☐ *Further Chronicles of Fairacre* **'Miss Read'** £3.95

Full of humour, warmth and charm, these four novels – *Miss Clare Remembers, Over the Gate, The Fairacre Festival* and *Emily Davis* – make up an unforgettable picture of English village life.

☐ *Callanish* **William Horwood** £1.95

From the acclaimed author of *Duncton Wood*, this is the haunting story of Creggan, the captured golden eagle, and his struggle to be free.

☐ *Act of Darkness* **Francis King** £2.50

Anglo-India in the 1930s, where a peculiarly vicious murder triggers 'A terrific mystery story . . . a darkly luminous parable about innocence and evil' – *The New York Times*. 'Brilliantly successful' – *Daily Mail*. 'Unputdownable' – *Standard*

☐ *Death in Cyprus* **M. M. Kaye** £1.95

Holidaying on Aphrodite's beautiful island, Amanda finds herself caught up in a murder mystery in which no one, not even the attractive painter Steven Howard, is quite what they seem . . .

☐ *Lace* **Shirley Conran** £2.95

Lace is, quite simply, a publishing sensation: the story of Judy, Kate, Pagan and Maxine; the bestselling novel that teaches men about women, and women about themselves. 'Riches, bitches, sex and jetsetters' locations – they're all there' – *Sunday Express*